PARUBHUMI

Anand Bihola

Made with ♥ on the Notion Press Platform
www.notionpress.com

To

That Special Moment

which ushered the Notion of this Story

to me

Author's Note

It has been one year now since I am in Parubhumi. As I have experienced and believe, all writers might have a similar kind of experience and feeling about their creation. A special moment comes to you with a notion or idea which itself starts telling you about it and you feel that everything to be your own thing, whatever it tells you. And you then get along with it.

I remember I was walking on the lawn near the patio at my home and that special moment transpired. I was thrilled with the central idea that special moment introduced to me. And then as always happens one by one all the characters started knocking on my door and a couple of them entered forcefully as well.

Parubhumi being the period story and the background of it being the Great Himalayas, I couldn't resist spending a little more time with the people of Parubhumi! But I remember how I was called back from Parubhumi every day by Leo, my son with four legs and a tail. He would put his front legs on my laptop or papers I used to write on and would remind me of his evening walk with me.

In all, it has been a wonderful journey writing this book. Of course, as it happens with all of us, I too had ups and downs in my personal life during this period. But those ups and downs too had their contribution in writing a few incidents in the book. Maa Saraswati as always kept showering her blessings on me throughout this creation. And as she does sometimes, this time as well she provided me with such actual tangible help while I was working on the second and final draft and I am grateful for that.

Lastly, I feel like coming up with the second and conclusive part of Parubhumi. I can't see all the nice people of Parubhumi confined to the small village. Moreover, it is imperative to free the land of Parubhumi from the centuries-old curse.

You are welcome to Parubhumi...

Anand Bihola

CHAPTER ONE

And again! It was third time now, and Vasudha was exasperated.

"This is too much Mahi, why you all are harassing me? Don't you know I am getting late and all of you are already done" Vasudha told her best friend Mahi with immense irritation in her tone. Mahi and the other girls were standing behind Vasudha close to a pond.

Vasudha was trying to apply *chakal* in her eyes while looking at the reflection of her face in the pond. The pond water was crystal clear and also calm as mountains around.

"None of us is doing that Vasudha, why don't you believe? We too know we all need to get ready on time for the festival *Pooja* and dance" said Mahi with an equal amount of irritation in return.

"Then who is harassing me again and again? As soon as I start to apply *chakal* in my eyes, someone disturbs the water and I can't see my face properly due to the ripples then" said Vasudha who was seemingly really annoyed.

"Okay, let us all watch around and try to find out the offender" all the girls said almost together.

"Meanwhile, if you wish I can apply *chakal* in your eyes" Mahi offered. It was second time she was offering that actually.

"No, I will do it myself, because none of you do it the way I want it" said Vasudha with a pinch of arrogance in her voice.

And only then came several voices from couple of girls around.

"Hey.. hey.. there.. see.. it is there, he is doing it, he is throwing the berries after eating them half, see.. see.." everyone looked up at the tree branches.

There was a mountain macaque sitting and devouring upon berries up there. It was sitting on one of the dense and higher branches of the tree. It was a berry tree which had grown abutting to the pond, half of it was shading the pond, leaned downwards.

"See.. see he threw it again" the girls said.

And they all then started hooting loudly and shooed away the monkey finally.

And on that moment there came a loud call from far away, someone was coming there running, "Hey girls... where are you all...? All are waiting for you...*Pooja* is to begin soon, come faster." He was Bali who rushed to call them up. He literally got exhausted wording that much. He leaned forwards a bit and started breathing heavily.

Bali was a village boy with only one hand. But he was a hawk-eyed aimer. With stones, he could bring down even a single targetted berry from the hundreds of them on the tree! Hence people of *Parubhumi* often would call him Bali - the aimer. He was very much popular among all the village girls as he could aim and shoot any fruit on the tree with a single hit of a stone.

All the girls now were excited. They were all in a hurry especially after Bali came there. Vasudha, finally with pretty reluctance, allowed Mahi with her flower make up and little bit of dressing as well. Half of the girls had already started walking with Bali towards the village. And after Vasudha and Mahi joined them running from behind, they all started rushing to the village place making sound ripples now.

It was the annual *Pooja* day for the village *Parubhumi*. They all were gathering at the Holy Stones field for this occasion of worshipping their supreme credence - The Mother Nature. They would worship Mother Nature's five basic elements today with hundreds of years old rituals. And those five elements were the Sky, the Earth, the Water, the Fire and the Air.

"Where are the girls yet? It is about time" said an aged man who was standing in the mid of a small bunch of men waiting.

He was Neharla, the headman of the village Parubhumi.

"There they are, they all are darting, see..." one of the men, standing and waiting for the girls to come just like many of him there, pointed towards one direction and everyone looked at that direction.

Finally, all the Girls arrived hastily. They all were dressed well, wearing colourful clothes, flowers and stone ornaments as well.

As soon as the girls reached there, Paataali started instructing them without wasting a second even. She was looking piercingly at girls with a scolding sight. Girls had made it so late though. She finally had a last gaze at all the girls' dressing and entire look. She lastly elucidated girls about the proceeding that was to take place shortly and also during that what girls have to precisely do. All the girls were so excited that they listened only half of it and rushed to the centre of the Holy Stones field.

Everyone there at the Holy Stones field was waiting so much eagerly for the girls to come there. As the annual *Pooja* proceedings could only commence then. Upon reaching of all the girls there, Hanula instantly started the proceedings. He asked five girls to come forward. The girls were given a white long cotton string and after chanting of holy hymns by the man standing in the middle, that string was tied with five earthen pots. Each pot was depicting one element of Mother Nature. Flowers were showered on them by men and women standing around. All bowed their heads to those five earthen pots.

While chanting the Holy hymns, Hanula made a slight indication to the girls to pick up the pots and hold them on their heads and start following him.

All the villagers then followed those five girls who were carrying one earthen pot each. They started heading to one of the deepest valleys of *Parubhumi*, into which there flown a river. All those five earthen pots were then to be submerged in that valley river. After reaching to the ravine of roots, all the five pots were put down in a round there, bound by that string. Then Hanula, the village pujari, again started chanting the divine hymns with eyes closed. Then one by one each of the five girls came forward and dropped the earthen pot they had carried here with their own hands. Then trees, some of the animals viz. cows, buffaloes, sheeps and goats also were worshipped.

And after completing the rituals, all the villagers returned to the Holy Stones field and they took appropriate seats with exuberance, as the annual dance function was to commence there.

Today's dance performers were awaited eagerly by everyone there. There was a unique wooden stage, exhibiting beautiful Himalayan flowers and petals of various trees. The girls were to enter from back of the stage and start performing.

Sitili, the in-charge of annual dance function there, quickly presented demo about the first few dance steps to the girls. All the girls were watching that meticulously.

But Vasudha was not at ease for a moment even. Her eyes were wandering all the time, as if looking for someone. She was quite reluctant to enter the stage. Couple of her friends however knew whom she was looking for. And at last even the music started playing.

"Vasudha it is event time now. I too have searched for him but he is not anywhere around here" said Dwija hurriedly, dragging Vasudha by her hand.

Finally, with much dispiritedness, Vasudha joined her fellow dancers and entered upon the wooden stage.

It was the dance about paying homage to the Mother Nature herself. All the girls were dancing in tandem with music. All the five elements of Mother Nature were portrayedby the girls turn by turn in the dance performance only. Vasudha wasn't able to concentrate on dance and while dancing even, she was seeking around every now and then and hence wasfrequently missing the dance steps.

The dance finally ended and everyone cheered and applauded delightfully.

On completion of that, the preparations started for the *Usa*. Itwas always the most awaited and cherished event in the annual *Pooja* function. *Usa* was a ritual cum competition of selecting the seventh *Walaha* every year.

Mostly the young men of village would compete for the *Usa*, however it was open for all men of any age. It was a time bound competition testing various survival skills and capabilities of the competitors wishing to get selected as *Walaha*. *Usa* was a very special contest in a way as there was punishment for the losers! And that way it was deliberated to make the competitors believe how important and crucial it was for a *Walaha* to be competent and capabale of overcoming obstacles and challenges successfully.

This year there were five contestants namely - Udit, Govind, Saral, Kala and Parjanya were competing to be the seventh *Walaha*. Udit and Saral had been *Walaha*s before, Govind and Kala had failed couple of times in past, whereas Parjanya was competiting for the first time. So it was only Parjanya who was inexperienced among the others. They all were so much excited and waiting and so was the crowd in the Holy Stones field.

All the other six regular *Walahas* were also there. Kadrula was the senior most among them. He was engaged in the last minute preparations of the competition. The level of hurdles and challenges of *Usa* had always been designed by the regular *Walahas* which mainly included the challenges and hurdles the *Walahas* would come across during their annual journey.

The participants were expected to negotiate the challenges chiefely connected to land, water and trees. Finally, all five competitors were called on and instructed to stand in a straight formation. Kadrula then stepped forward and explained the competitors about the rules. Though all of them were well versed with the rules, yet they listened and understood it carefully since Kadrula was speaking! It was a competition with time limitations and time was a key and decisive factor at the same time and all knew that. Finally, the wait of the crowd and competitors came to an end. They all were set, waiting for the bird call to begin the race. And there it was! A golden Oriole gave a melodious sweet call and all the five started running at once. It was a long distance and vast area, almost entire village, for them to cover with different challenges. Hence one regular *Walaha* was present at each significant point to watch over the competitors.

They first would come across the sloppy lands followed by water streams and tree trunks. All the people gathered there cheered loudly for the five. Vasudha had also come there; she was still looking for someone though. And there he was! Running! Vasudha too cheered loudly along with her friends there. That was a matter of few minutes only, since all the competitors had almost faded away running but it was real excitement all over among the spectators. A huge crowd was watching their heroes. All gathered there knew that it would take hours for the competitors to reach to the final hurdle at the Uni valley. So as soon as the runners disappeared, many of the crowd started for their home for the daily chores to complete. However, they were walking hastily to finish them up and getting back to the Uni valley to watch the competitors crossing the final and most difficult hurdle.

It was almost the evening and finally all five were seen at the Uni valley. They all were wet, muddy and bone-tired but still running with all the remaining strength. All of them were at little distance from each other, however. Udit was at the first position, followed by Kala and then Parjanya, Saral and Govind. They all came to the last and most challenging barrier which was the artificial wooden bridges made over the small cornered patch over Uni valley. Though this was merely a competition but the last challenge of crossing the bridges was a real serious one, as the bridges were having no side supports and were covered with ice as well. Moreover, they were only two human feet in width. Hence there was a high risk of getting slipped off and falling deep down in the valley. The whole crowd was watching now with high breath. As Udit was the front runner, he went to the place where bags filled with various stuffs were kept. In this last stage of competition, the competitors were required to carry such stuffed bags with them while crossing the bridge and that would make the last hurdle the most difficult and dangerous as well. Udit reached to the bags and he quickly picked up all the five bags one by one, putting one on his back, one each around his arms and couple of them holding in his hands only. He then started running towards his bridge but it was evidently difficult for him now to run freely with that much weight. Meanwhile, all the other competitors too had arrived there and they too had started picking up their bags kept there. After Udit, Kala started on his bridge. After few seconds, Parjanya, Saral and Govind too were on their respective bridges loaded with heavily stuffed bags. The spectators were not cheering now, but they were a little excited and worried. All the current *Walahas* too were there, watching this. The competitors who were running hard and fast upto now, were now putting each step pretty carefully! At the same time, they were avoiding looking down deep in the ravine. Kala had staggered for couple of times just in few steps and so did Saral. Udit was still ahead of them all on his bridge, walking slowly but with confidence. But among all of them, Parjanya was much confident and quicker, he had got tremendous balance of his body while walking with weight even. He walked down the ice bridge quickly and finished as the winner. Everyone watching was astonished with the speed and swiftness Parjanya showed while crossing the ice bridge. From all sides, people were cheering the victory of Parjanya. He was tremendously happy that he couldn't stop his tears. And how he could have? It was his dream to go on the annual *Walaha* trip with his role model and hero Kadrula. And he had made it.

And none but Kadrula himself came to him and said "Well done Pajanya. You have proven the excellence. We are all proud of you". And then one by one Bhola, Tatu, Velu, Buma and Haja all the other regular *Walahas* came there to meet and greet Parjanya, their new ally. Parjanya was accorded the wooden stick by Hanula as the mark of felicitation.

And after the annual *Pooja*, dance and *Usa*, all the villagers had the feast together. Sweets made of fruits and milk were served to all in abundance. The villagers had a great time and they really enjoyed the day and thus the annual function was concluded. In conclusion of the event, the Pattika also felicitated Parjanya. And as every year, the unsuccessful competitors knew that they would have to stay outside the village for next three days on their own. But at the same time, they knew that it was more a future training, rather than a punishment.

CHAPTER TWO

Parubhumi was a unique village. It was an isolated and lonely village in the ever untouched parts of the great Himalayas. On its East, was the deepest ravine, the Ravine of Roots, as it was called. It was called so because there were numerous small rifts and ravines within it. And the exact opposite to it, on the West, was the greatest and most stalwart, the *Busa* Mountain. People of *Parubhumi* revered *Busa*. However, *Busa* was separated from the *Parubhumi*'s mainland by a very deep rift. On the North and South were the Uni Umi valleys. *Parubhumi* was a blessed as well as cursed land at the same time. And it was a village with very limited population. But it was a completely self-sustaining village. Most of the village requirements were met with from within the village itself. But some staple food grains and certain medicinal fruits and plants had to be brought from outside to grow and plant every year. And it was because the land of *Parubhumi* was cursed! No seed which was grown on the land of *Parubhumi* would be useful as sowing seed for farming. So everytime new seeds were required for the farming and other medicinal plants and fruits. And for that purpose only, every year selected seven men would go out of *Parubhumi* to fetch the required medicinal plants, fruits and necessary grains seeds to sow and those seven Men were called the *Walahas*. Six of them were chosen by the Mother Nature herself. There were fixed rituals for selecting the Permanent *Walaha*and those rituals were as old as *Parubhumi* itself. Such rituals were based mainly on the timely omen signs from the Mother Nature. The *Walahas* were much respected people among the other village people. The seventh *Walaha* had to be selected by a competition among the village men every year. Only ten living people were there in the village at present who had gone out of the village borders. *Parubhumi* was having very less plain and evenlandusefulfor cultivation and farming. And such flat cultivable land too was only in small patches around the village area, mainly separated by small hilly and rugged lands as well as small water streams and ponds.

People of *Parubhumi* knew absolutely nothing about the outer world and about the other human habitation, if any, on this planet. Every year only seven men would go out of village and distant, crossing the ice bridge that used to be formed naturally every year with snowfall in the hard winter over a very particular narrow spot at the ravine of roots.

The *Walahas* would go to the far-off parts of Himalayas to fetch the seeds of *Sothi* – the main food grain of the people of *Parubhumi,* along with other necessary medicinal plants and medicinal fruits growing there as well as a few other saplings for plantation, and that too, with the rituals that would allow them to go out only if there were pious omen and signs that are indicatively proper while performing those rituals.

Faith was the one word which could describe the human character of people of *Parubhumi.* They would always be faithful to the law of Mother Nature. There was a Holy Stones field there in *Parubhumi*; plenteous stones with different shapes were in there. Any important gathering, public meeting and social or religious functions of *Parubhumi* would take place at the Holy Stones field only. Neharla was the village head and extremely respected aged man. He would manage the life in general of the people with the help of other men and women of the village.

Apart from the village head, for any important decisions and guidance there was the *Pattika*. A committee of elderly and experienced men of the village. Neharla was the second most aged person in *Parubhumi*. After him, Kadrula was another respected person. He was the senior most *Walaha* since years. Kadrula had remained unmarried just to serve the Motherland *Parubhumi* with his full dedication! Hanula was the chief of religious and spiritual matters. He was the village *Pujari*. His forefathers and ancestors once had been where he was now. And after him was Jhanula, he was the chief of public health. He knew every single plant and petal and their medicinal and wellbeing use for humans as well as animals. He would look after people and animals' health in *Parubhumi*.

There were only a few things such as Home and clothes which were owned privately by the people of *Parubhumi*, rest majority of the things and stuffs were general and of public ownership. People of *Parubhumi* would work for their village and village people and not for their family merely. Farming and animal husbandry was cooperative entirely. Each particle of grown grains was village property and would be divided and distributed among the families of village proportionately as per the number of family members. Village artisans would work for village people and not as individual professionals. The requirement of essentials had to be informed to the concerned artisan, and such requirement would be met within due course of time. No extra goods or stuffs were produced to be stored. The main livelihood of the People of *Parubhumi* was of course animal husbandry but farming also was equally essential. In *Parubhumi*, women would always be playing equal role at every front and would share responsibilities in social as well as economic activities. Since having quite limited population as work force, the role of women was prime at every front in fact. Birth of child would be celebrated with immense joy as a general festival. Every such new comer would be considered as Mother Nature's property and would be treated as her gift.

Children were taught basic life lessons as well as crafts and arts in the village *Gunali*. Experienced elderly men and women would visit there on days allotted to them and would teach the children about the life lessons as well as important things for sustenance at *Gunali*. Girls were taught cooking and weaving along with other skills exclusively by elderly village women.

CHAPTER THREE

All the *Pattika* had gathered at the headman Neharla's home. They all were sitting there and having hot milk served by Paataali, mother of Vasudha.

They all had gathered there to discuss and plan this season's *Walaha* trip. Yesterday only, Parjanya was selected as the seventh *Walaha* for this year. So he would be joining with the regular six *Walahas* for this year's annual trip.

The Pattika was glad for Parjanya as well. Hanula, Jhanula, Kadrula and couple of other elderly men were the part of *Pattika*. "Parjanya is the descendant of the greatest of greats, he would definitely go a long way as *Walaha* in the years to come," Kadrula said with so much complacency on his face. Everyone agreed to that without any doubt.

"He has all the qualities of becoming a regular *Walaha* as well, like his great great grand father" Jhanula added in praise for Parjanya.

"Okay let's now decide the day for this year's annual journey of *Walahas*" Neharla came back to the point.

"We can do it on day after tomorrow, as it is the very portent day as per current stars' position" Hanula said.

"Okay then, Hanula… kindly prepare for the *Parama* on that day. The bridge is ready and we should not waste more time now" Neharla added. And then he looked at Kadrula and said "Kadrula you and Jhanula should discuss and prepare the list of necessary things to be brought from this trip. And kindly bring more fodder seeds this year as the summer would be a little shorter this time, I guess".

"As you say Neharla. We both would work out and calculate the requirements of various necessities" saying this Kadrula looked at Jhanula who just smiled and nodded his head. And after discussing a few other things about routine issues, they all dispersed.

Neharla then went inside home and called for Vasudha, Neharla's son Virajla came out and informed his father that Vasudha was not seen around since morning so most probably she must be somewhere with her birds.

"Now on the left shoulder," Vasudha ordered Bali who was ready for second time, with the stone to be thrown and hit the man standing distant who was rubbing his right shoulder after getting hit by a stone there already.

That man was alone there and watching out the grazing cattle of the village. But he was now looking around to find who was hitting him with the stones. And then only, he again got hit on his left shoulder.

"Next on the butts" Vasudha was getting more aggressive, as if she was not at all satisfied yet.

"No no please, no more now, poor Parjanya is already hit badly three times now, just let him go, stop here please" pleaded Bali.

"No, not yet, he should be taught a lesson that he remembers for a longer time, come on, aim again" ordered Vasudha.

Vasudha and Bali were hidden behind a big boulder. They were on the upper elevated land portion, from where they were able to see Parjanya easily but for Parjanya, it was difficult to locate them from where he was. So he was just looking all around in quick successions.

Bali then quite reluctantly said "Okay, let me find some more stones then" and he moved little away as if trying to find more stones. He moved hiding even further away, and then suddenly, Bali within a moment ran away from there.

Vasudha was stuck looking at the running Bali. She, for a moment, thought to call him loud, but at very next moment she realised that it would only expose her to Parjanya. So she helplessly kept watching Bali going away. So then, angry with two persons at a time, she herself looked for some stones and to her immense surprise, she found few of them right there only that Bali had left behind. 'So Bali cheated me!' she thought. Liar..Thinking that she picked up one of the stones, the bigger one in fact, she carefully aimed at Parjanya and hurled it with her full strength. But it missed by a mile!

Vasudha immediately got down and hid herself.

"Oh I see, Bali has gone now, I think" said Parjanya loudly from far and then laughed.
Hearing this, Vasudha got up from behind the boulder. She was still very much angry. And while walking to Parjanya, she aimed and threw couple of more stones at him which Parjanya very easily negotiated with. She went closer to Parjanya and tried to hit him even from there, which Parjanya saved himself from and again laughed loudly.

"You.. you.. scoundrel.. you.. How dare you didn't come to watch my dance" Vasudha was fumbling with words due to anger and Parjanya kept laughing.

"You miss a lot.." finally Parjanya said slowing down with laughing.

"Yesterday while dancing too, you were missing the dance steps a lot" he said with big smile on his face now.

"So you were around? Where were you? You were watching me? Really?" asked Vasudha still annoyed.

"Yeah, I was watching you only" said Parjanya with smile and trying to hug Vasudha. But Vasudha got away a little and asked,

"But then why hiding? Why? You know how eagerly I was looking for you all the time around?"
"Yeah that's the very reason. For me it was far far better that you look around for me, than you keep looking at me only while dancing" said Parjanya grinning again.

"You know how embarrassing is it for me? I still remember the last year annual dance function, you just kept looking at me all the time" he added.

"So what's wrong in that, I dance only for you there" said Vasudha.

"No, you should be dancing for Mother Nature, keeping her in mind only" said Parjanya.

"Of course I dance for Mother Nature too" Vasudha corrected and then asked immediately, "How was I looking? Did you see those flower hairdo on my head? Was that all good?"

"Yes you looked beautiful as always" said Parjanya. And then ran to one of the buffaloes that went close to the nearby rift and took it away from there.

"Yesterday Udit was here on the duty and he saw a snow leopard, so I need to be careful" he told Vasudha coming back to her.

"So what have you eaten since morning?" asked Vasudha as ifnot contended with praises from Parjanya.

"Hmm.. okay yeah, one Apple and three stones" Parjanya replied smilingly as always.

"Oh did they hit hard? Is it still paining?" Vasudha asked with much concern.

"Oh nothing, I was just joking".

"Okay but tell me, did you have proper breakfast today morning? As I have told you to have on the duty day" asked Vasudha sternly.

"No actually, sorry, but yeah I had handful of butter you gave me last time" Parjanya said.
"Oh butter? It is still there? Means you don't have it regularly" said Vasudha with disappointment and irritation.

"Parjanya, please take care of yourself, your food, there is no one to take care of you at home and you have to take care of yourself as well as your great great grandfather" Vasudha became little emotional.

"Oh dear, don't you worry this much please. I am fine. Just look after them for a while" he pointed to the grazing cattle, "I am just coming back" saying this, Parjanya ran behind one big boulder to the bushes nearby. He came after a while with two big fruits in his hand. He gave one to Vasudha and other he started eating.

"This was the favourite fruit of my mother" he said emotionally, "so I eat this, especially when I am damn hungry and miss my mom. She would always chop it for my father and put in *Tirka* as well to make it spicy but she would always ask me to eat this whole only" his eyes got wet.

Vasudha said "Yes you have told me this before" she gave him a hug, and while parting she said, "Your mother is around here only, as my mom says, nothing is beyond this universe, nothing can go out of it. It is only about the distance. We have our limitations regarding distance, but who knows, once we die and become part of the greater Soul, we wouldn't have such limitations of distance". And after rubbing Parjanya's eyes with her *upaalu* that she was wearing, she said "Come home for dinner tonight, would you? or else, I will send grandpa to fetch you".

"No no, I will come, it has been a long time since I had loaf and butter from Paatali maa," said Parjanya.

Both then kept eating the fruit, which was just like a smaller version of the Sun above!

CHAPTER FOUR

As every year, the winner of *Usa* was to be ritually nominated as *Walaha*. Many of the villagers gathered there for that unique ceremony. Parjanya was the man today. He was dressed in all white as part of the tradition for this particular day. It had been his dream since his childhood which was going to be the reality sooner now.

Every year, after the annual ceremonial *Pooja* ritual, the *Walahas* would leave for their annual journey to fetch necessary things from Mother Nature. *Parubhumi* was blessed with so many special and unique things, and that small village was a self-sustained village. But yet some special medicines and grass plants to grow more grass for the cattle had to be brought from some distant places of the great Himalayas.

The village pujari Hanula was there in the centre along with Neharla. A big circle was made there with flowers as its borderline. A newly born calf was brought there along with its mother. Both the calf and its mother were offered *Pooja* first, they were worshipped by Hanula. Parjanya had one piece of cloth on his upper torso and another one on the lower part of his body. Hanula asked him to stand in the centre with him. He entered the circle and stood accordingly. Thereafter one small grass bundle was given to Parjanya.

He was very much excited as he didn't know what next to do and how to do that. He simply was following the instructions of Hanula and sometimes Neharla, who also was just around. Now Hanula put an earthen pot full of water up to its edge on Parjanya's head. And he was told not a single drop of water was to be dropped on earth during the process. Suddenly Parjanya became little serious. He was standing like statue thereafter.

And then, Hanula called the mother cow forward along with her calf. The cow entered the circle but went to other direction, so all were tensed a little as the cow was supposed to go to Parjanya who was holding grass for her.

All were watching with so much eagerness.

Hanula was watching as if nothing had happened. The calf was just walking by its mother.
The cow then kept moving around for sometime without even looking to Parjanya. But still she hadn't crossed and went out of circle. And that was important as well. The calf too was following its mother every step.

Finally the cow came to Parjanya and started eating from Parjanya's hands, and only then the calf started feeding itself from its mother's breasts.

"There it is" said Hanula and Neharla at once simultaneously.

"Parjanya is accepted by Mother Nature as *Walaha*," declared Hanula.

Everyone gathered there, cheered up for Parjanya. Hanula congratulated Parjanya. And all the other regular *Walahas* as well cheered for him from away.

Vasudha was also cheering from far away, but even though Parjanya's eyes caught her. She was looking so much happy.

Then Parjanya was taken to all the current six *Walahas* who were present there in the ceremony.

Kadru, Bhola, Tatu, Velu, Buma and Haja all the six *Walahas* congratulated their new ally.

Immediately Parjanya was taken to the Sira river for the holy bath. There Parjanya had to jump into the river from the height of almost 50 meters. Parjanya was taken to the edge of one big rift and then Hanula did tilak on his forehead. Everyone started waiting for some natural sign then. As per the traditions of hundred of years, all the auspicious things would be commencing only after the omen sign, mostly any Bird's or animal's call or any other natural sound.

After the silence of few seconds, there was a loud thunderstorm sound from the sky. And at once Parjanya jumped into the deep valley into the Sira river as prior instructed by Hanula. Everyone cheered that loudly.

Sira river was considered to be the most pious river among people of *Parubhumi*. It was said that the very first dweller in *Parubhumi* had come there crossing the Sira river only. And that primordial Saint used to go and take bath in Sira every morning. It was the rite and belief that the one selected as *Walaha* has to cross the village boundary for the very first time via Sira only.

After having the holy bath, Parjanya could come back after half an hour. He had to climb and cross many small rifts. After Parjanya came back, Hanula offered him the especially made garland, which he always will have to wear then on when going for annual journey. Parjanya was the youngest among all the present *Walahas*.

On the very evening Parjanya was at Vasudha's home. Neharla was also very happy for Parjanya for being accepted as *Walaha*. Vasudha's mother Paataali was serving food to all the three men having evening meal. Parjanya, her husband Virajla and her father in law Neharla.

Vasudha was making hot loafs made of Sothi – the special and staple grain of *Parubhumi*. Somehow Vasudha was applying more butter on hot loafs today than any normal day. She too was very happy today. Because it was well believed that the person accepted as *Walaha* was always the choice of Mother Nature and that person would be the pious one.

While eating, the three men were talking about today's occasion.

"Kindly tell me what precautions I need to take in order to not breach any law and terms of Mother Nature when I would be out with other *Walahas*?" Parjanya asked politely to Neharla.

"Kadru is the most experienced and oldest *Walaha* among all of you; of course, he will guide you as you are new. But still a few things that I did learn when I myself was *Walaha*, which I can tell you. The first and most important thing is, to respect Mother Nature and each of its creatures. Each of them I repeat" Neharla told Parjanya. "Always walk into the steps of the front men walking ahead of you, unless it is some natural emergency. Whenever you take or pluck anything, just let know or ask Mother Nature first, she never denies anything, however" Neharla said further.

"I will keep all this in mind Neharla" said Parjanya politely.

Parjanya had very much respect for Neharla, since his childhood was almost without parents and had only great great grandpa who was unable to speak listen and see, so Parjanya was like a member of Neharla's family. Neharla too had a very special place for Parjanya in his heart.

"I was a kid when your great great grandfather was *Walaha* leader, he is considered to be the best *Walaha* of all time till date Parjanya" said Nehrala.

"Oh, my great great grandfather too was a *Walaha*? I didn't know this up to now" said Parjanya with surprise.

"Yeah he was, unfortunately, he has lost all his senses of speaking, listening and seeing, else he is the man as old as this village in a way," said Neharla.

"I am very happy for you Parjanya, I myself have tried for selection as *Walaha* in past couple of times, but I couldn't be. This is the highest honour to serve our motherland *Parubhumi*" Virajla told Parjanya. Viraj, who would always prefer to be silent and work but on this occasion, he couldn't resist to show his true happy feelings for Parjanya.

Then three of them finished up with their meal and after sometime Parjanya left from there. It was still ice cold atmosphere despite the season of winter was ending.

Upon reaching home, Parjanya as every day, lightened the earthen lamps and started to prepare milk for his great great grandfather hastily.

This milk, along with some herbal roots, was the only meal for Shivala since decades.

Parjanya took the roots of one of the Himalayan herbs to mix it in the milk. The herb was kept at its daily regular place. But upon touching the herb root, Parjanya found it recent wet.

He in a moment had gotten who might have come here in his absence. He went to see his great great grandpa's room; Shivala, his great great grandpa, was fast asleep. And beside his wooden bed, there was a bangle, a wooden bangle with colourful stones onto it.

And Parjanya knew that bangle so well.

Next day Parjanya was ready to leave by the sunrise. This was his dream morning infact. He had taken all that what he was told by Kadrula as well as Hanula to take with him.

He went to his great great grandpa's room, which, as always, was dark. Parjanya kept on seeing Shivala for quite few moments. He kept on looking to the man, whose voice he had never heard, whose eyes he could never look into, he would talk to him but always knew that the words were never to reach to him. He got somewhat emotional. He just had heard things about his great great grandpa's unique abilities from the veterans of village, but never had seen those things being done by him. All Shivala was able to do was getting up only twice in a day, does his daily physical things with someone's help and, drinking some water, having milk at the dinner and again going to the same motionless condition for hours.

Parjanya offered his homage to Shivala from away only. He also offered homage to his late parents at the same time from within and came out from Shivala's room. He stopped at one particular spot in the courtyard; he had very faded memory of his mother feeding him food here when he was just a kid and always would want to go out to play with other kids, eating only half what he was served. Parjanya stayed there for a while as well and then left.

He knew very well that each day someone from village would come and take care of his great great grandfather.

In few moments he was with his fellow *Walahas* in front of the Rift of roots. This was the rift through which all the *Walahas* used to go out of village once in a year since centuries. And the miracle about this rift was, every year, there used to form a flat narrow ice bridge that would combined a small and narrow portion of two deepest rifts together and that too only when the harsh winter was gone. That bridge would get melted just in a week or so and hence the *Walahas* had to get back to the village by then anyhow. This bridge would thus enable the *Walahas* to cross the great rifts rather easily than what they would have to without it. Since that was the only way to enter the *Parubhumi* too.

Hanula gave each of the *Walaha* a small wooden stick, and did them *Tilak* on their foreheads. All the *Walahas* kept that wooden stick on their right shoulders holding with left hand and kept waiting. All were waiting for one thing and that was one of the fixed omen. There was a pin drop silence for quite some time, and then came a call from Himalayan Golden Oriole!! As prior instructed by Hanula, all the *Walahas* started walking on the ice bridge one by one. And thus the annual *Walaha* journey got flagged off.

CHAPTER FIVE

Vasudha opened her eyes; it was morning, though the Sun had not arisen yet, morning was always her most favourite period of time of any day.

As usual, Vasudha had woken up by the chirping and singing of birds. She got up from the bed and went outside. It was her favourite season as well. Birds were singing and calling. There were so many birds around. They were flying here and there.

Some were flying so high in the sky as well. And they were the migratory birds as Vasudha had learned this from her mother. 'They would go far distant places', her mother used to tell her. "Far? How far? Where?" Vasudha would ask.

'That I don't know' mom would say. And that curiosity had led Vasudha nurturing her love for birds right from her childhood, because birds could travel, they could go places wherever they want to, she used to think and would get fascinated with that notion.

Birds always had been her friends and she used to sit and watch them for hours, watching everything they do.

And suddenly she remembered that today for the first time, Parjanya was not there at home and even in the village. He had gone away, far far away. Like birds, yeah, she thought.

"Oh, so you have already started doing it right from early morning today" Paataali had come there.

Vasudha looked back to her mom and gave her a good morning smile.

"See, they have started doing their daily rituals and chores" Paataali said coming closer to Vasudha who was sitting on a small Rock and was still watching birds doing their morning things.

"I know mom, few more minutes please" Vasudha just pleaded to her mom.

"Okay dear, but we need to prepare breakfast for your dad earlier today, because today he is to go to farming work in place of Kadrula, who has left as *Walaha* yesterday" Paataali said and left a bit hastily.

After few minutes, Virajla, Vasudha's father, along with three other men, waiting for him, left for the farms. They all started off with the same amount of enthusiasm Vasudha had been witnessing since her childhood for this particular season of the year. It was the beginning of the farming and plantation work in the village.

In *Parubhumi*, there was village farming. No land was of anyone's personal. All the lands were village land and farming was all village farming.

Everything whatever grew would be stored and distributed among all the village families as per the number of family members.

In fact, most of the things in *Parubhumi* were like the way farming was. They were public in spirit and not anyone's private.

It was the time to prepare the small pieces of cultivable lands for farming. Plain lands in *Parubhumi* were in small patches mostly, scattered around the village. In fact plain lands were really scarce in *Parubhumi* because of its being situated in the mountains area. And only plain lands were cultivable lands, useful for the farming. In that too, due to the harsh weather, especially the winter, the lands needed to be reclaimed every year. Lands would become hard like rocks, hence they first needed to be ploughed and made softer at the upper crust. Every year, in this season, these land patches needed to be re-prepared for sowing, as the *Walaha*s would bring with them new plants and seeds for farming.

There were several water streams around the village. So water harvesting as well as artificial waterways were made to drive and fetch the water to the fields and farms. Virajla was the man who had that expertise. He had designed and planned the artificial water waterways in such a natural way that the original flow could also be kept intact when the water wasn't being used for fields and farms. So it was only after the harsh winter is over, the artificial waterways were made activated to reclaim and cultivate the farming lands.

As always, it was a week's time only for the people working on the land preparation task. It was a rule not to undertake any activity relating to farming before the annual *Pooja* ceremony. And after the annual ceremony only, *Walaha*s could leave for the trip in next couple of days. So every year the land and farming work would have to be so much time bound and hence each villager, men and women would work hard equally for that.

So all the young and mid age men were busy in land cultivation and farming related work these days, along with their permanent activity that was animal husbandry, cattle grazing.

Parubhumi was a self-sustained village in all manners in true spirit. And the concept of everything belonging to the village-people was the soul of this self-sustenance.

Each expertise, be it farming, or medical treatment of human or animals, water usage, civil work, or religious and spiritual things, everything would be passed on to generations to generations and everything was just for the well being of the village and for the well being of village people only.

For Vasudha, today was very slow day she was feeling, and that's how it became a very long day for her as well. She went to the root-valley, which was the farthest and the best place in the village according to her and also one of the boundaries of the village. But yet Vasudha felt that time was not passing by normally somehow. She was habituated to be with Parjanya during certain time of a day, so now when Parjanya was away, she felt so much empty and restless.

"So you are here again, where are you going again? Or just wandering around? asked Mahi.

"No, actually I am looking for Dwija, but not finding her around, so trying to find her at every possible place" Vasudha replied and tried to get off from there.

But Mahi immediately held Vasudha's by her shoulder and said "Hey, I know, but it's only the first day dear, I know he is out for 7 days and that is a long time, but you have to wait, okay? He has gone for well being of all of us".

"Yeah I know, but I am not finding respite anywhere" said Vasudha half heartedly.

"I do understand dear, okay, i need your help. You know our Gauri had a strain in her front leg, so let's.."

"What? When? she was dancing so well in the annual *Pooja* day couple of days back only, when did she get that leg strain?" asked Vasudha surprisingly.

"Oh no, not our friend Gauri, she is all well, I am talking of our cow Gauri, she got the leg strain so let's take her to Jhanula for the treatment and then let's go to the fruits farm and work there. I know it's not our turn today" said Mahi just stopping Vasudha saying something in between.

"Okay I will join you after lunch" said Vasudha and left from there hastily.

"So here we are" said Kadrula, the leader *Walaha*, stopping at one dense Jungle place and putting down the baggage he was having on his back.

One by one all the other six *Walaha*s also stopped there after reaching there, as they all were walking on the foot steps of their leader, keeping some distance one after the one.

"Look at that" said Kadrula to Parjanya, pointing towards a huge tree just besides.

Rest of the *Walaha*s knew what was there. But for Parjanya it was new.

He looked up and got amazed. The tree was a huge one; he never had seen such huge trunks of a tree in *Parubhumi*. There were wooden boxes placed safely between branches on that huge tree. Parjanya was just mesmerised seeing such huge giant thing in a tree form and shape!

One sign from Kadrula, and Buma climbed up that tree and brought down the boxes with the help of other *Walaha*s. All the boxes were place safely and then opened up.

There were huge pieces of clothes in there along with some wooden torches and other useful necessary things for their journey ahead. Everything was taken out of boxes safely and placed appropriately. They all then started working on the things that they took out from the boxes. And after couple of hours' skillful hard work, they made tents out of them, it was late evening by then.

Velu had gone somewhere and after sometime, came back with ample fruits and nuts of different varieties, some of which Parjanya never ever had eaten before or even seen before.

It was all surprise for him there.

"So we will spend the night here and will start again tomorrow morning" said Kadrula.
Except Parjanya, everyone else was having years of experience so they all started preparing for the night in their respective tents. Two of the *Walahas* were to be watchmen till the midnight, and then another two were to be the guards after midnight till morning. So it was decided among them without the directions from their leader. Bhola and Tatu were to watch and guard the area after midnight, so they already went to sleep as early as possible, in order to wake up at midnight and watch till morning. Velu and Buma were to watch till midnight.

Parjanya just kept looking at the people and things happening around him as if some pre-defined automated system. Except Parjanya, everyone else had this business every year, so they were quite normal with doing such things in sequence one after another. Parjanya didn't know how to make a tent, so he kept looking at his collegues working around him and helping eachother. Finally, Kadrula himself came to Parjanya and taught him to make a tent. Parjanya kept following what Kadrula was asking him to do. And after few minutes, Parjanya was in his nice warm tent made by himself.

However Parjanya couldn't sleep even after getting in his tent for quite some time. He kept thinking about Vasudha, Shivala and *Parubhumi*. He still would pinch himself to assure himself that he wasn't dreaming; and he really was out and far away from

Parubhumi. Everything here was like a dream. He finally got out from his tent.

It was much colder outside. After walking few steps, Parjanya saw Velu coming from one direction holding burning wooden torch in his one hand. Parjanya went closer to Velu, so Velu after greeting him with smile, asked "Couldn't sleep, right? Happens, it's still new to you so it is normal. But after couple of such trips you would be attuned to all this" he said.

"Yeah, tried but couldn't sleep so came out" Parjanya said, and looked around. Parjanya started walking along with Velu.

"Why it is needed to watch around? For the snow leopards?" he asked.

"Not only the snow leopards, but mainly for the bears; they sometimes become dangerous" Velu said.

And then only came Buma from the opposite direction holding the burning wooden torch in his one hand just like Velu. He too had the same question to ask about Parjanya.

"Couldn't sleep, right? Then join us, and in short time you would start feeling sleepy" he said and all three of them laughed.

Kadrula too was up and watching them talk. He asked for Parjanya when three of them were passing by his tent.

"Kadrula you too are still up?" Parjanya asked surprisingly.

"Yes, come, sit with me" Kadrula told Parjanya with so much affection.

And then Parjanya was up till late night, and so was Kadrula.

Kadraula wanted Parjanya to know and learn everything, as it was his first trip as *Walaha.*

Both talked a lot. Parjanya asked so many things regarding this *Walaha* legacy and other rituals being observed in the *Parubhumi.*

And when he went to his tent to sleep it was almost dawn. But he had learnt and known such things from Kadrula that had convinced him about *Parubhumi* being the most pious land on this earth and almost each ritual and rule the people of *Parubhumi* followed was only and only in order to respect the laws of Mother Nature and to respect the other living beings and ecology around.

CHAPTER SIX

"It is almost done, there you go, yeah very good" Vasudha was feeding Shivala.

After Parjanya left as *Walaha*, everyday one villager would come and look after Shivala for his morning needs, in the noon and at late evening, as decided.

Though Vasudha knew it very well that Shivala, more than couple of centuries old, had lost his senses of hearing, speaking and seeing, but still she was talking to him today as she knew Parjanya would always do that.

In a way, she was talking to herself. And she was very happy today as it was the day when the *Walahas* were to be back.

"Shivala, our Parjanya is coming back today, all *Walahas* will come back today" Vasudha said, while laying Shivala down on his wooden bed after feeding him the glass of milk.

All Shivala could do, and was doing was, just looking at her, but not at her actually. But had Vasudha seen into his eyes properly, she could have seen that Shivala was replying and responding to all what she had told him till then.

Vasudha left from there after finishing her job.

And while returning to her home, she could see everywhere there was enthusiasm among the village people, in fact there was enthusiasm in the atmosphere itself, or was it just because she was happy? She thought and smiled.

Almost all the plain fields and lands were being ploughed and made ready for sowing. Every year the place or field of the one particular crop was changed and different crop seeds were planted and sowed every year. People were working to make space for new plantations as well.

Vasudha just stopped there to see all around; in fact she had witnessed almost the same scenario for years now since her childhood. Water streams were being guided through specially made artificial waterways to reach to the fields and farms.

It was still pretty cold though the winter had recently left. And this was the time Vasudha would always love. Numerous birds would fly over the sky to reach to their destinations. Many of them would visit *Parubhumi* for short break as well. And Vasudha would be so happy to see them every year.

Vasudha went to her most favourite place, the Rift of roots. It was the deepest and largest Rift, having so many small rifts inside it, and thus providing homes for thousands of birds and other creatures there.

Vasudha used to spend hours there at the Rift with birds and their calls and other activities. She always felt that the Rift of roots and the *Busa* both were a couple in some way. Vasudha sat on a boulder of her fixed choice place. And as always she started thinking about Parjanya only. What he must have seen, would he be feeling same like her? Keen to see her, meet her.. and only then, came Mahi there.

"Hey Vasudha, I looked for you everywhere, come, the *Walahas* would arrive within hours now. Everyone is eager to receive them. Hanula and Neharla are leaving to come here to receive them, preparations are going on for rituals, lets join them and then come here back" said Mahi in one go and she started dragging Vasudha with her.

There, Parjanya was also walking with great joy and excitement. Velula who was walking just ahead of him had to look back twice and ask Parjanya smilingly to maintain even distance as the other *Walaha*s were maintaining. He had already once told Parjanya that maintaining even distance was important in order to keep vigil eyes around. Parjanya would feel shy and again slow down himself. He was *Walaha*, he still felt immense joy and surprised of it. Mother Nature chose and accepted him from among others. And he had now seen so many things in this great Himalayas, new lives, animals, trees and new medical fruits and plants and what not?

He too was thinking about telling Vasudha everything what he had felt and what he had seen and so many things. But one thing he decided to tell Vasudha for sure and it was that, the simple looking man Kadrula, was in fact very knowledgeable and intelligent man. Not just that, he was the man who knew everything about the laws of Mother Nature.

Once, when a mother snow Leopard with her cubs happened to cross their path and got angry and hyper in the situation, how Kadrula handled the situation and avoided any confrontation with her, convincing her about they are not going to harm her or her cubs. How Kadrula would pluck the fruits and seeds while chanting hymns. How he would be alert for saving himself and other *Walaha*s from any possible threat and at the same time not at all thinking of harming anything in front of him and so on.

Parjanya too had learnt chanting hymns for taking anything from the trees since long, but he now realised that Kadrula even knew the language of animals too. He could convey the other soul what he wanted and meant, and that too, silently!

As it was not allowed for *Walahas* to talk while they walk, hence Parjanya had to let go off so many questions and curiosity by now during this journey. But one thing he would always do as taught by Kadrula on the very first night halt of this journey, and that was, to observe everything, and observe it silently.

"If you observe properly, you will have all the answers for everything about Nature" Kadrula had taught him.

They all were walking and walking continuously, with so much lesser rest breaks now. Somehow Parjanya felt that he wasn't tired even he was walking for long hours during the return journey. And while walking, at one of the turnings, Kadrula stopped, and so did all other *Walahas* one by one. All put down their baggage off there back and relaxed after their leader did so. Even while taking the break like this, all the *Walahas* would keep maintaining the same even distance they would do while walking. Only during the meal time and at the night halt they would get together at one place.

"So, we are now close to our *Parubhumi*. We need to cross that small mountain only" said Kadrula. There was a mixture of emotions of happiness and satisfaction on his face while saying this to all the other *Walahas*. Another annual *Walaha* trip was successful under his experienced leadership, and he was happy for that.

They all then drank water from the nearby water stream, rested for a while and after some time; again they all got going in the same manner. After walking much distance and even closer to the village, once, Kadrula suddenly stopped again, so did rest of the *Walahas* one by one. Kadrula very carefully looked around the path and then that particular patch of land twice. He bent a little more to the ground for couple of times. All the *Walahas* were watching him with eagerness. Kadrula kept observing the path with some seriousness and then he looked back to the other *Walahas* watching him, so he smiled, and again started walking.

But somehow Parjanya felt that the smile from Kadrula was not the smile actually. Something was there which Kadrula avoided to share with other *Walahas*.

At the evening time, the *Walahas* were seen at the Uni and Umi valley. But as per the geographical situation they had to walk around to reach to the Rift of roots Snow Bridge. The snow bridge actually was combining the two deep but close rifts which were parts of the Rift of roots itself. And this snow bridge would make it possible to cross the ravine of roots that easily and get on the other side and in fact outside of *Parubhumi*. And these two were the deepest rifts, so deep that their bottom land was never to be seen up to now. But even after the winter had passed, and when all the other snow around *Parubhumi* would mostly meltdown, this Bridge would still last for another 10 days, and that too in the air! And it was since centuries that this was happening. So its sole purpose was that only, the Annual *Walaha* trip.

And this snow bridge would meltdown just after exact ten days. So it was necessary for *Walahas* to get back to the *Parubhumi* by then. Moreover, it was also much risky to cross the snow bridge while returning, because as the time passed, the bridge would become little thinner and hence would not be as strong when it actually got formed.

And that is how years ago one *Walaha* had lost his life while returning and crossing this snow bridge. And so it was the emotional and nervous time for Parjanya.

As the leader, Kadrula entered the snow bridge first; he was walking as if he was walking up to now throughout the journey. However the snow bridge was hardly two human feet wide and that too without any side protections, but Kadrula had crossed it for so many times and he was just like that everytime. Then one by one Haja, Bhola, Buma, Tatu, Velu and Parjanya all did it with real care seemingly on their faces. Moreover all the *Walaha*s had held the bunch of bags filled with stuffs in their hands and on the backs as well, hence the maximum care of balancing and for not getting slipped off was needed.

The *Walaha*s were welcome as per the rituals. Hanula had taken back all the small wooden sticks from the *Walaha*s carefully while chanting the hymns. They all were made sit in a circular manner and the holy water pot was kept in the middle. Then the water from the holy pot was sprinkled on all the *Walaha*s and only then they entered the village.

As every year, the *Walaha*s had brought the medicinal plants and fruits for humans' as well as the animals' use. They also brought some saplings to grow there in the village. And also seeds of different plants and grains to grow in the land of *Parubhumi.*

Since *Parubhumi* was cursed only for one thing, and that was the land there couldn't grow its own seeds once again, hence every year the *Walaha*s had to bring new seeds and plants for plantation and farming and that too in big quantity. In fact almost ninety percent of the total stuffs were that of the Sothi seeds only.

Once the *Walaha*s entered the village, the helping team of young men from the village took over the burden of stuffs brought by *Walaha*s. There were different types of seeds and plants. Everything was segregated and placed safely in the village *Bhandaras,* in the custody of Neharla.

The village *Bhandara* was a wooden godowns, where the agricultural crops, medicinal fruits and plants and other commodities were stored for the use of every living being of *Parubhumi.* The godowns were almost in the back of the open land of the village near the Uni valley. One huge godown block was further partitioned forming other smaller godowns. Each of them was covered with special roofs made with grass to protect the commodities from snow and rain fall.

As soon as Parjanya got free from all the proceedings, he hurried towards his home. He was away from his great great grandfather for 7 long days. And this was for the first time in his life up to now. He reached home and saw that Shivala was sitting on his bed as if waiting for him only! Parjanya went to him and sat by him, and told him that he was back, he knew that his great great grandfather was not at all able to listen to him, but somehow Parjanya had always felt that Shivala sees, listens and understands everything but he wasn't ready to communicate with anyone anymore.

And at that night, Parjanya was with Vasudha. He gave Vasudha few flowers that she never had seen and few fruits that she never had eaten before.

"I told you not to bring anything from there, still you didn't listen me and have broken your promise" Vasudha was unhappy with Parjanya.

"No I haven't broken any promise" Parjanya said with smiling face.

"So you had told Kadrula that you were bringing all these for me?" Vasudha with some hopeful manner asked Parjanya at once.

"No" Parjanya just said.

"Then how could you say you haven't broken any promise? Parjanya please, this is against the law of *Parubhumi.* We both know..." Vasudha just stopped saying anything further.

"Yes I know, my dad had done this for my mom, and people say that's why he lost his life while crossing the ice bridge"

Parjanya said in a much unknown voice, unknown even to Vasudha.

"But one thing I am sure about now is, my dad must have broken any of the rules of Mother Nature, any basic rule yeah" he added. There was silence for a while.

Vasudha then came closer to Parjanya and took his one hand into her hands and said "I am sorry Parjanya, please forgive me. I didn't intend to remind it to you hurtfully. Believe me please."

"I always believe you Vasudha, I know you care for me and that's why you are telling me all these. But you please believe me; I haven't broken any rule of Mother Nature and brought these here" Parjanya said lovingly, looking straight into the eyes of Vasudha.

He then told Vasudha everything about his journey as *Walaha*, his experiences, about places, trees, animals and especially birds and everything. And Vasudha could see what Parjanya had seen, and she could feel what Parjanya had felt about everything during that journey.

CHAPTER SEVEN

There was a loud bang on the door and Parjanya opened up his eyes at once. As he was away from home and had been among the jungle and unknown places for past few days, Parjanya at first couldn't make out where he at that moment was. It was dawn. But soon he realised that he was in his very well-known room and not amidst the trees and rocks in the jungle. Yes he was back yesterday only, he assured himself. And he was sleeping at his home; he realised and breathed deep in relief.

It must be a *Bhor Rukka*, he thought, the man who would wake up people in the early morning at stipulated time, people who needed to wake up early in the morning to go for work in the early morning hours. And that was the routine arrangement in *Parubhumi*.

And since, it was Parjanya's turn today to go for the village cattle grazing duty; the *Bhor Rukka* had banged his door to wake him up. And he would do it to so many others today as well, Parjanya thought while leaving the bed. As from today, the farming and plantation work was to be commenced since the *Walahas* had come back with all needed seeds and other plants.

Parjanya went to Shivala's room. Most of the time, Shivala was with closed eyes, but as his own ritual, Parjanya would always first see him, and then only would go out of home every morning.

And after finishing with his daily morning routine, which included Shivala's needs and routine as well, Parjanya was on his way to the village cattle shed and other animals' sheds. He was happy to be back on his most favourite job. He had always loved the company of cows and other livestock. He would take great care of their every small need with his deep understanding about that. On his way to cattle shed, he could see men going in numbers for farming and plantation work.

"*Aajo*" Parjanya greeted all of them, and received the same response, with '*Walaha*' as prefixing his name now. Men would plough and sow the seeds. And that crop would feed the whole village for one whole year. There were different land patches of different sizes throughout the village. And all would be cultivated for different crops and plants. Separate land patches were segregated for the cattle fodder as well.

Suddenly Parjanya stopped and touched the soil he was walking on; he touched it with so much respect and gratitude in his heart. He himself couldn't understand why he did so at that moment. But he did it with much gratitude, that's what he was feeling right in that moment. He stopped for a little while and then again moved on.

He had to take a turn from the medicinal fruit farms to go to south as the Uni valley was just there and and so were the sheds, it was also one of the village boundaries as well. Parjanya loved the Uni valley because just after that his revered mountain *Bora* was situated there. However it was not as big as *Busa*, but it looked so much like a great human being. The father mountain, he would call it. Parjanya had not seen his father well because he died when Parjanya was just a kid. But whenever Parjanya used to miss his father, he would go and sit in front of *Bora* for hours silently, and sometimes with closed eyes, and would feel like sitting with his father only.

He reached to the cattle and other livestock shed. As soon as he was opening the wooden gate, all the cows started mooing, and thus making a great sound as if they were welcoming Parjanya. They knew that their friend was there after long time, so they were asking him to let them out as quickly as possible. They all knew Parjanya so well. And when Parjanya opened the gate fully, all the cows one by one, and some together as well, passed by him touching him with their heads and rubbing their bodies with him. They always had loved Parjanya as their caretaker.

Prajanya knew that all the cows always knew where to go, once they are out. So he didn't bother to lead them, and then he went to the nearby shed, which was shed for sheeps and goats mainly. And he found the same loving response and treatment there as well. All the sheep and goats were out and they too knew where to go. All of them were rushing and running. There was a different grazing field for them though.

And there came Adhu and Buka. As Parjanya was walking and following the herds, he met with this duo. These two guys were always together wherever they would go. There wasn't a single incidence when any of the village people had ever seen either of them alone.

They greeted Parjanya and told him that it was time to trim the sheep and take off the wool, as the winter had gone. So Parjanya needed to bring back the sheeps little earlier. Parjanya told them that he would surely bring them earlier today and moved on. Adhu and Buka were to take off the wool from all the sheeps and then the same was to be handed over to the team of women headed by Gokali, wife of Velu. She and other women and girls would make woollen sweaters, mufflers, bed sheets and top sheets out of it.

Parjanya knew the exact numbers of cows and buffaloes as well as the sheep and goats, so he needed to count them only when he takes them back in their sheds. Parjanya was feeling so much complacent after being back on his favourite job. He had been with these animals for almost two decades now. As part of the rotation system of the village work committee, everyone in the village, irrespective of man or woman, had to work in every required area turn by turn. So every man and woman of *Parubhumi* was having the required skills, and in that way they were supporting the one village family community.

But in all of these, Parjanya had always inclination towards the cows and other livestock grazing job. He would take extra care of these animals, would even talk to them and listen to them as well. It was said in the *Parubhumi* that 'whenever it was Prajanya's turn for the cattle grazing job, the animals would always give more milk than the normal days', and therefore Parjanya in fact was given more days of duty at the cattle grazing job!

In the lunch time Vasudha came to him. She had brought lunch for Parjanya as always. For Parjanya, the lunch was always from Neherla's home. Either Vasudha or his mom or dad would bring it or would send it with someone or sometimes Parjanya would go to have it at their home as per his that day's duty and job times.

"I was expecting that you only would come with lunch today" said Parjanya taking clay containers from Vasudha.

"Yeah couldn't see you properly last night as it was dark, so" said Vasudha smilingly and looking into the eyes of Parjanya while handing over the buttermilk clay pot to Parjanya.
"Those were the longest days of my life" she added sitting by Parjanya.

Parjanya just looked at her and smiled with affection. He unfolded and opened the containers one by one and looking to the food said "Oh but didn't you think this is too much for me?"

"I too am going to eat with you, so brought my food here as well" said Vasudha and fed Parjanya the first morsel with her own hand.

But before Parjanya could eat that properly, suddenly there was a loud and painful cry by one of the cows grazing little away from there.

Both Parjanya and Vasudha got startled.

Parjanya got up and ran to that direction with big strides, and Vasudha too followed him.
"Be careful if snow leopard is there, Parjanya" Vasudha was saying while running behind him.

Upon reaching to that cow, that was still in pain and was trying to take her one leg out of some grass patch there, Parjanya thought it was some animal that had been there but he could see nothing there except a strange colour grass amidst which that cow had put her one leg.

Parjanya went so close to that tangled leg of that cow, and to his immense surprise, it was only that strange grass that had grasped that cow's leg, and that strange grass was making some low witchy noise at the same time.

Vasudha reached there as well, and she too looked at that closely. She too was immensely surprised and shocked a bit.

Parjanya at once took his stick and winched into that strange grass. And he was again surprised to see that the grass grew up a little in a fraction of second after the stick had hit it.

Parjanya was very much scared now. He threw away his stick and immediately held the tangled leg of that cow with his both hands and tried his all strength to pull it off. At once Vasudha too joined him in pulling the cow's leg off that strange grass.

The cow itself too was toiling hard to take off her leg from the grass. She was screaming more and more at the same time as well.

"Please stay away from the grass Vasudha" while pulling Parjanya warned Vasudha.

And finally three of them could successfully pull off that entangled leg. The moment that cow's leg was out of the hold of the grass, the cow ran away, and it ran away with so much fear. She was bleeding badly, Parjanya and Vasudha could see the blood trails on the ground.

Both were so much shocked that, for couple of moments after the cow's release, they couldn't understand what had happened and what was to be done now. But first Vasudha got up and went to the direction where that cow had gone.

The leg of that cow was still bleeding and there were deep scratches on it. The cow immediately ran far away from there too. And wasn't letting Vasudha to come closer to her. It was very much frightened indeed.

During all this time there was a commotion amongst the other cows and they all started mooing loudly.

"You go to village and inform Neharla immediately, I am coming with all the cattle just behind you" Parjanya told Vasudha.

Vasudha ran towards the village straight away.

And Parjanya started gathering all the cows at one place and away from that strange grass patch.

There was still very much fear and commotion amongst the cattle, and they all were mooing loud one after another. And at the same time they all were mooving fast here and there.

First time in his life as a cattle caretaker, Parjanya felt that Cows were not listening to him and in fact not trusting him for the time being. He still wasn't able to figure out what actually had happened.

At the same time Parjanya had to take care that the cattle moving here and there in fear don't put their feet again in such strange grass. He went to check that grass patch again and it was really a strange thing he felt.

It straightened up a bit the moment Parjanya reached closer to it. And started making lower noise and that was very sharp and piercing noise indeed.

Parjanya got much frightened seeing that. He went back to the cows again and patted them and tried to comfort them.

And after few minutes all the cows encircled him coming closer to him as if they were sorry for how they behaved with him for sometime.

And then came the village people.

Govind and Saral were among the top speed runners, followed by other Village men.
"What is that what Vasudha was saying" asked Govind and Saral almost together breathing heavily.

"It's something really strange, It is there, come" Parjanya led both of them closer to that strange grass patch.

And they were joined by Mohan Buma Velu and Kala soon, they all too had come running and hence were breathing heavy.

They all kept staring at that strange looking grass. It was indeed some dark grass.

"And where is that injured cow?" asked Mohan.

"It is there, still bleeding" Parjanya led him to that cow.

All rushed to the cow. Its skin was badly damage and got off the bone. Blood was still dripping from the fresh deep scratches.

And then came Neharla along with other elderly men of village, including Jhanula.

Jhanula immediately started treating the injured cow. He applied some green paste on that cow's wound. That cow was still so much scared and agitated that she wasn't allowing anyone except Parjanya close to her. She wasn't at ease and was moving here and there.

Neharla went closer and looked at the dark grass closely, and he just said "Oh.."

Kala also came there; he suddenly picked up a big stone and threw it fiercely on to the dark grass.

And immediately the dark grass responded with sharp witchy noise and also grew and spread a bit as well.

All the villagers including their head Neharla were very much scared hearing to the witchy noise and especially the quick reaction the witch grass had shown.

Neharla asked Kala not to do anything to the dark grass, he was unhappy with Kala's reaction to the grass.

Mohan took away all the cows, the sheeps and goats from that area and led them back to the village.

And rest of the men just gathered there little away from the dark grass. They all were scared as well as worried very much.

"How come such an evil looking thing has come up on the land of *Parubhumi*?" Hanula asked, as if asking himself only. He had come there lastly in fact.

"I haven't seen such thing in my entire life" said Kadrula still looking to the far away dark grass patch. Kadrula came there just before Hanula.

Neharla was still sitting quiet, looking down.

"What we do now Neharla" Kadrula asked worriedly.

"Nothing, let's not disturb it, just stay away from it and be careful. It may go away on its own" said Neharla. But all present there felt that Neharla himself didn't have that trust in his those words even.

They all were terrified and were looking at the dark grass as if it would chase them down and catch them. No one was speaking. All of them one by one again went closer to the dark grass and observed it with some unknown fear.

Finally Neharla, the head, asked Kadrula and Parjanya to put little bigger and medium size stones and boulders in front of the dark grass edge to form a boundary to stop it spreading further to the village direction.

Everyone helped putting small and medium boulders and stones in a row and in a circle form to control the dark grass spreading further to the village.

And since it was evening, Neharla asked everyone to go back to village. Everyone with heavy hearts and worriedly left for the village.

Parubhumi had always been a very happy and prosperous land. People of *Parubhumi* were having very limited requirements in terms of their daily life. People of *Parubhumi* were always having immense faith in Mother Nature. They never would see anything as offensive neither with any sort of animosity to things around them whatever it was. Everything belongs to, and is from Mother Nature only, was there basic belief.

However they had got frightened by the emergence of the dark grass, it was something that they were really not habituate to. Fear, and hatred getting originating from fear, was not at all something that was at all known to the people of *Parubhumi*.

And still things were changed. People were not feeling free on their own lands now. Mothers had confined their kids to the limited areas of the village only, and so was the case with the young boys and girls. People while walking on land were not feeling it safer now.

As instructed and requested by Neharla, the village people had continued with their daily work, as they couldn't afford to lose this important time of farming and plantations. But they all were not at all at ease for a moment. Men and women again and again would go and check the dark grass in fear.

And after couple of days only, the news came that the dark grass was seen in the west and north directions of the village as well. And that was the real worrysome news for all of them. Up to now Neharla had tried to assure them all that the dark grass would vanish on its own and Hanula too had started some special process with the chanting of hymns everyday. But emergence and spread of the dark grass in other directions and areas of the village had scared the village people even more now.

As decided, the Pattika and other village men were going to see and check the dark grass where it was first seen. It was still there! Had grown little further, and it was still there, firm. All went closer to it to see it properly. It wasn't grass certainly, that's what they all felt. It was something really strange. They all again sat a little far away from it. Jhanula looked at Neharla and said "We have to do something to destroy this evil grass Neharla. It won't go on its own anyhow, we have to destroy it".

"But how can we destroy anything like this, and that too, just because it is a threat to us? It is not harming us unless we come in contact with it" Neharla reluctantly said.

"I think Neharla is right, Jhanu. How can we destroy anything which is created by Mother Nature itself, even if it is kind of evil in nature" Kadrula supported Neharla.

"But it is growing and increasing, it will be stronger with time" Govind said with great caution in his voice. Couple of younger men at once supported him.

"You are right Govind, let's wait for some more days, we may decide after that" Neharla said.

Everyone got back to the village, though act of the dark grass was just kind of an enemy, but people of Parubhumi, especially the elderly people, were still having their beliefs and faith in Mother Nature and its each creation.

All they were possessing along was one thing, and that was Faith, sheer Faith! And life in *Parubhumi* was going on with it, within it.

CHAPTER EIGHT

All the men of the village had gathered at Neharla's home, as he was the headman of the village. They all were in a deep worry and thoughts. No one was speaking. And that was because Bhola and Tatu two of the senior *Walahas* who were sent to check that dark grass patch and any effect of those boulders and stones which were placed to control further progress and spread of the dark grass and they reappeared with the disheartening news.

The dark grass had taken over the boulders and covered them completely. Not only that, it had grown a little taller as well during the night.

Parjanya came there a little later. He must have run to reach here, as he was gasping when he stopped.

Each eye present there looked at him with so much hope to hear some comforting and positive news.

"Neharla it has started growing in the east too" Parjanya said with drowning voice. And saying this he dropped down on a small boulder there.

Back to back saddening news made all present there sunk in deep sorrow. Men started talking in grim voices with one another. Today morning, on Neharla's instructions, the cattle were sent to southern side of the Village so as to keep them safe and away from the dark grass. Mohan and Govind were sent with Parjanya today, so that three of them can have better help of one another.

"I have asked Govind and Mohan to watch over the cattle and have come to inform you" said Parjanya, as if trying hard to stop himself from breaking down.

"Now what?" Jhanula asked, but no one was having its answer.

"Viraj, You and Velula please go to the southern side up to Uni, and Bhola you and Tatu please go up to Umi in the North to check whether that dark grass has emerged there or not" Neharla told in a plain tone without looking up even.

And all of them stood up and left in different directions. Neharla again slipped into thinking. Being the most experienced man, no one ever had seen him this much tensed ever.

Vasudha, who had come with her mother Paataali to serve the men hot milk, also was looking so much worried and for a second she looked at Parjanya, and in that blink of eye she could convey Parjanya that things will be fine.

Parjanya took the hot milk pot but didn't sip. In fact no one did. All were waiting for Virajla, Velula, Tatu and Bhola to come back. No one talking. It was a heavy silence there.

They came back. And they were having the same sad news. There were patches of dark grass in the Northern and Southern sides of the village too.

"But how is that possible, yesterday only I had been there at Umi and there wasn't any such grass there" Govind said with great amount of surprise in his tone.

Couple of men also said the same, they had been to the eastern and western parts of village yesterday only and they had seen nothing like that they informed.

All of them started talking with fear of unknown. No one knew what was going to happen now.

"We are being surrounded Neharla" it was crying voice from Saral.

"Something has to be done urgently, else we all would be in great peril and danger" said Bhima, looking to Neharla, who was seemingly in deep thoughts. "We have to destroy that evil, now no other way is left for us" Bhima further said looking to all men gathered there as if seeking their say and support in this.

And before Neharla could say anything, Hanula stood up and said "I think Bhima is right Neharla. We should destroy the dark grass now. It is time, yeah" Hanula, as only on certain occasions he would do, said in that fashion.

Neharla looked up, first to Hanula, and then looked at Kadrula, Kadrula was silent too. But as if Neharla had understood, he said "Okay, if there is no other way out to control the dark grass and its evil acts, let's destroy it".

All the men got up in excitement as if waiting for Neharla to lead them to the dark grass.

"We can burn it out; Fire is one of the purest forms of Mother Nature, that would be the best way to destroy the dark grass" Hanula suggested.

Right away wooden fire torches were made available. They were set on fire. Hanula held one in his hand and one was held by Kadrula. All of them went to the dark grass patch which was seen first in the pastured area. The village people were happy to see them going to burn the dark grass and also because Neharla finally had agreed to destroy the evil grass.

After reaching to the dark grass patch, Hanula went ahead of Kadrula. He stood near the patch and started chanting the Holy hymns for a while and then without an iota of hatred or any bad feeling for that creation of Mother Nature, he put the fire into the dark grass as if he was releasing and relieving it from something.

But in a moment the dark grass engulfed the fire itself. Everyone there was stunned seeing that. Hanula too stepped back in fear and shock. All there were shocked too seeing the reaction of the dark grass. Kadrula quickly went close to Hanula and threw his wooden torch straight into the dark grass patch. But in fraction of second, the dark grass got tight hold of it and started squeezing and engulfing it too. All present there got frightened so much. They walked back, little away from there. The dark grass had no effect of fire! Not only that, it started making its witchy noise too. Kala and Bhima together picked up one big boulder from far away and they ran to that patch and threw the boulder with full strength to crush that dark grass patch. But the dark grass got hold of that big boulder as well, as if it was some grass bundle! And in few moments, it started crushing and engulfing it.

Every one was terrified seeing that. All moved little more away from that patch now. They were so much shocked that their lips were sealed.

"Witch grass" Neharla said, as if saying and confirming to himself only.

And every one looked at him astounded.

Neharla was looking at the patch while uttering these words with his eyes wide open.

"What? Witch grass? What's that?" asked Kadrula as if couldn't understand.

"Yes, witch grass this is! I don't remember much of it since i was a kid then but i had heard of it. This is witch grass" Neharla said in quite different voice and tone. He started walking back to village even without looking at anyone standing there.

"I really remember nothing of it now. But yes I have very faded memory of its being deadly. And like these days, our parents too had confined us going out of homes and playing in open" replied Neharla to Kadrula who worriedly asked Neharla if anything he remembered about the witch grass of his time.

All had gathered at Neharla's home after coming back from that patch of witch grass. Everyone fell into the deep thoughts, all were tremendously worried.

As if came back to the present moment, Neharla looked up and said "More or less it's all about what Mother Nature wants, nothing else. What we can do, we would do, and rest is her choice and verdict. Come on, let's all have milk please" saying that he started sipping from his container.

And after everyone had finished with the sweet warm milk, Neharla told everyone present there to continue with the daily fields, farms and other works. And to take proper care while they move around. He specially asked Parjanya and Bhola to take care of the cows and other livestock and asked everyone to be at the Holy Stones field after the dinner late evening.

Everyone left from there to do their daily job then. And they had perceived one thing vehemently, and it was, Neharla was the man of mettle. In that testing time of great danger too, he could keep calm and could make others feel that things would be alright. Everyone left from there with high respect for him.

However it wasn't easy for the people of *Parubhumi* to ignore the threat of witch grass and live normal life. It was also because the witch grass had now started making witchy noise quite frequently, as if laughing at the people who were in a way being surrounded and getting under siege. Women and mothers of small kids were not allowing their children to play freely in the village lands. They were under the constant fear of unknown threat lurking just around. As the women of *Parubhumi* had always contributed in all day to day socio-economic activities at par with men, the children were all on their own in so many ways. So now children too were feeling the heaviness of some unknown due to which they were being confined.

As always Holy Stones field was lightened by earthen lamps. Any ritual or important gathering or anything important was always discussed at this place in *Parubhumi*.
Almost all the men had come but still Kadrula and couple of other men were awaited.

In normal times, such gatherings were always so much exciting and cheerful. People would talk to one another about variety of things going to happen and so on. But today everyone was silent and down, some sort of heaviness was prevailing all around there.

After Neharla, Kadrula was the most senior and experienced man in Parubhumi. He was ideal for every young man of *Parubhumi* actually. Neharla had many times expressed his will to leave the headmanship in favour of Kadrula, but the Pattika, the other important people who were holding the important place in the society in *Parubhumi*, had declined and kept requesting Neharla to continue.

Finally, Kadrula came there and took his vacant seat just next to Neharla.

The atmosphere was still chilling, though it was the end time of the winter now.

Atmosphere among the men gathered there was also chilling, mixed with some unknown fear, no one was speaking. And anxiety and fear were mixed with that silence.

Neharla looked far end and back and finally said, "We all villagers of *Parubhumi* are in an unknown danger. As we all know the vicious witch grass has started growing around our village. It is much far from the main village land right now but it is inching closer day by day and growing taller as well. It hurts and kills whatever it catches. I heard of it when I was merely a kid I remember but to my misfortune, I don't remember anything more than that. But the fact is, if we had survived in our time, it means, there must be some remedy of this witch grass to deal with and survive".

"Shivala is the man who must be knowing about this witch grass" Kadrula said looking first at Neharla and then at Parjanya, who, instead of sitting like everyone else, standing a little away by a lamp.

"Yes Shivala must be knowing about this witch grass but how would we get that information from him? He can't hear and can't speak. We are helpless" said Neharla with disappointment.

"But he can see yeah", Kadrula said with some hope, again looking to Parjanya.

"Yeah he can see a little bit at times I think" said Parjanya from away, looking to Kadrula and then Neharla.

"Then we can take him to the witch grass and show him that and see if he can somehow recollect and tell us something about that" said Kadrula with much amount of hope now.

People of the village gathered there now started talking to one another in some hope and excitement instantly. They suddenly started feeling that someone was there who could be helpful to them. For the past few days, people of *Parubhumi* had been so much depressed and hopeless that any kind of small hope or possible help had made them believe that there was still a way out of that peril situation, and they would survive.

"Okay, then tomorrow as Kadrula says, let's try that way if Shivala can help us or if Mother Nature wants to help us through him" said Neharla.

And he then, addressed all present there again "Our *Parubhumi* is a sacred land of Mother Nature. We will fight and defeat this witch grass but till then we are not going to stop our daily work. Those who are with farming and plantation may please continue with their work properly. Those who are on duty for cattle grazing have to take great care of the cattle. Let's bring Shivala to that witch grass there and see tomorrow" saying this, Neharla stood up and so everyone else did. With the hope as high as then dark looking *Busa* far away, people of *Parubhumi* left from the Holy Stones field.

CHAPTER NINE

So many eyes were looking at one man's eyes, but those two eyes of that man were just looking into blank! He was looking nowhere with eyes open!

With pile of high hopes, Shivala was brought to the witch grass area in the South, where *Busa* Mountain could be seen. Today Shivala left the village after decades in fact, he was brought there along with his wooden bed. With great efforts he was made to see the witch grass from very close distance, the witch grass that had grown further in terms of area as well as height.

So many of the villagers had gathered there. They all were wishing the same one thing - Shivala to see and recognise the witch grass. They all knew that Shivala was their only hope in terms of getting any way out of this life threatening situation.

But Shivala, even if while looking at the witch grass, wasn't looking at it in fact. As always no one could find out and understand what he was looking at actually.

Kadrula tried to explain Shivala so hard that finally he broke down in tears, even then Shivala didn't understand him. Seeing a mountain like man breaking down like that, was really disheartening for the villagers.

Parjanya was looking all these from a little distance. One by one Kadrula, Neharla and couple of other elderly men came to Shivala, sat with him on his famous wooden bed. They tried their best to talk and in fact explain Shivala with all their heart but Shivala was as always, an Idol! Absolutely no expressions whatsoever.

Parjanya was getting disheartened seeing all that. With heavy heart he walked a few steps and went to Neharla, who also was disappointed greatly, and told him something.

And after sometime, on suggestion from Parjanya, it was decided to leave Shivala alone there for some time, so that if he could sense something himself at least.

All went away but all were watching from distance, still hoping for the miracle to happen. Only movement Shivala was making was, of his hair, and that too not by himself, but by the wind that was blowing. Minutes passed, but nothing happened.

And then, Bali came there. He was looking so excited. He had one idea. He first went to Neharla and talked to him. Everyone present there got surprised for what Bali had to tell Neharla. Neharla listened Bali and then he asked Bali to go to Parjanya. Bali with the same excitement ran to Parjanya who had fallen in deep thoughts and was sitting, looking down. Bali called Parjanya with much excitement but Parjanya didn't look at him, so then he held Parjanya's hand and jerked him couple of times.

Parjanya, as if, came back to the moment, looked at Bali.

Bali, with even more excitement, started telling Parjanya what he had on his mind. Everyone there was staring at Bali with different sight since Bali was a non-serious type of young chap of village. But when Bali finished with his idea as well as excitement, even Parjanya too felt it little interesting. Parjanya stood up and went to Kadrula.

And then, as per Bali's suggestion, a stone was thrown on to one of the nearby and big witch grass patch where Shivala was sitting close by, as it was known that the witch grass would start growing just immediately after someone tries to destroy or disturb it. And at that time it would have movements and witchy sharp sound too. So chances were high that it could well be noticed by Shivala, as he was made to sit pretty close to one such patch.

As expected the witch grass responded the same way immediately, but Shivala didn't! Few more stones were thrown one after another with some pauses and intervals to give Shivala enough time to observe and realise. But all the efforts just resulted only into growing up that witch grass patch a little more and also making it more agitated.

Finally after 2 hours, Neharla asked Parjanya to take back Shivala as he had slept already. All of them came back to village carrying Shivala back and highly disappointed.

"If we can't stop this witch grass anyhow, it will surely destroy us all, by killing and engulfing everything" said Virajla.

"I think we all should move out of this place now" said Adhu.

"Yeah yeah that is the only thing remains now in order to survive, leaving this village" couple of men supported him instantly.

After getting back and disappointed by Shivala, the Village men had gathered at their headman's home as usual.

"Paataali was telling me that the cows and buffaloes are now not giving that much milk as they used to give prior. Today morning when Paataali along with other women was at the *Gaughar*, they could have lesser quantity of milk than what they usually were getting earlier everyday" said Virajla looking so much grim.

Now this was another issue of concern as Milk was one of the staple and main food commodities of consumption for people of *Parubhumi*.

"Whatever mother cows give us and whatever we make from it, is all the main part and portion of our daily food, it would be much difficult for all of us to sustain with shortage of it" said Mohan.

Everybody was telling issues and different situations to one man, their head Neharla, Neharla was still silent and sitting with his head down.

"Say something Neharla, after all you are our head, and after Shivala, you are the eldest man and hence most experienced too" said Tatu.

Neharla looked up at Tatu, one of the *Walaha*s, and with very sad tone he said "All I know and can tell you is we, the people of this great land, can never leave this land, never. I will let you all know about the reason at the right moment".

"But what is that which cannot let us move from this land, even when our lives are at stake?" asked Haja.

"I have only one answer of your all questions, and that is, I will share with you all when the time for that would come" said Neharla with some unknown tone.

There was a pin drop silence among the men there after that.The second most senior man also was fallen into deep thinking.

"Then it means that we have to have our way out of this problem, and we will have" said Parjanya, looking up the sky which was getting darker now.

"And if Neharla remembers such similar problem in past, and even after that if *Parubhumi* had survived, it means there surely must be some way out of this problem yeah, and Shivala is the only one who might know that" Kadrula said while sitting and still facing down.

And for few seconds the air there become hefty by number of silent sighs.

"I don't know much about this but since my forefathers and our dynasty has been that of the *Pujaris* of this village since ages, I think there might be some mistake or lacuna in proceedings of sending off the *Walaha*s or breach of any rule of Mother Nature by either the *Walaha*s or even by me. As only then such great calamity and danger can surface" said Hanula, the current village Pujari.

"In fact, I, myself too was led to believe this but couldn't share with you all, but now Hanula has said the same" Neharla at once said.

Few of the eyes were pointed towards Parjanya instantly. Parjanya felt so much embarrassed and to some extent convicted even, that he could not hold on looking at any of them. And no one else but Kala finally said "Among all the *Walaha*s, only Parjanya was the new and hence inexperienced one".

"But I haven't done anything against the law of Mother Nature, no, neverI can do, you all can ask Kadrula" Parjanya said with his whole heart.

At once Kadrula said "I can vouch publically for not onlyParjanya, but no other *Walaha* has done anything against the law of Mother Nature during entire last *Walaha* journey".

"I had expressed my point of doubt only, I didn't mean that this must have happened due to any kind of mistake from any *Walahas*" Hanula immediately clarified.

"Since Kala wasn't selected as *Walaha* by Mother Nature, he is trying to blame Parjanya just out of jealousy" said Saral. Few voices came out in support of this. And then there was just like a wave of distrust for Kala in a while. Other young men of village started hot arguments with Kala in favour of Parjanya.

Finally, Neharla stood up and said "Please calm down, please. Whatever the reason may be, now the demon has knocked the door, hence we all should trust Mother Nature that she would help us and guide us in this testing time. Our *Parubhumi* is a sacred land and we all have survived through ages, so let's go now and pray to Mother Nature. Those who have the duties of cattle grazing, farming and plantation would continue with due care"

Everyone dispersed with heavy heart from there for one more night.

CHAPTER TEN

"Listen please, listen to me Parjanya, I am not claiming that this has happened due to that only. It's just because today when I went to fetch water at the stream, I heard Gauri and couple of girls were gossiping similar, so I just reminded you. So please don't rush for Kadrula". Vasudha held Parjanya's one hand tightly, who was trying to get up.

"But now I too am feeling that this might be a strong possibility Vasudha, I must not hide this from our people. They all are at great peril and big risk on their lives only because of me I feel, just think of this" said Parjanya with so much pain in his voice.

"No Parjanya, please don't feel so, this is only a possibility yet, we can't say this is the only reason" Vasudha said tightening her grip on Parjanya's hand.

"That's why I want to share and confirm," Parjanya said stopping Vasudha.

"But please wait for some time, who knows some wayout maybe found out by then to destroy the witch grass" Vasudha said as if praying to Mother Nature at that very moment.

Parjanya got little calm; he sat down and again sunk into thinking.

Vasudha had reminded Parjanya about the flowers and fruits he had brought for her secretly from the far places of Himalayas during his *Walaha* trip. Parjanya had completely missed that incident from his memory and hence he could defend himself in the last gathering at Holy stone field. But now he was regretting hugely for that, he was feeling as if he had cheated everyone by lying that night by saying that he hadn't broken any laws of Mother Nature. He was feeling as if he had cheated his own people, especially Kadrula, Kadrula at once came to his support there when Kala put up the point of doubt, and he in way had cheated Kadrula there by not sharing and accepting what he had done.

It was Parjanya's duty today at the grazing fields.And as always, Vasudha had come there with breakfast for Parjanya.

Days and nights were not as ago in *Parubhumi* now. It was a nice winter ending yet sunny day but gloomy. A continuous grim and depressing atmosphere was prevailing there all the time. People would not talk with each other normally. In normal days, Parjanya surely would do some prank with Vasudha whenever she would come with breakfast or Lunch for him. And same way Vasudha too would do some trick to make fun with Parjanya. But time was changed drastically now.

After finishing with breakfast, both Vasudha and Parjanya had gone closer to the witch grass to observe it properly. They could see that the witch grass had been growing and spreading steadily. In the initial time there were some patches only. But with time, those patches had expanded and in some places and areas, they got merged and formed a big portion which looked daunting itself. Moreover it was making even sharper witchy noise than earlier.

Parjanya was looking at one such big patch. He was feeling so much grim thinking that if all such small patches keep growing with time and ultimately they were to get merged with one another, then it will be a circular formation of witch grass, encircling the entire village area and that would be something really really grave situation then. And the witch grass wasn't only growing horizontally but vertically as well. It had grown more than human ankle height now in some areas.

And only then a tiny but sharp scream distracted both of them.

He and Vasudha startled andlooked at that direction and ran there. One rock lizard ran away from the witch grass patch direction quickly, but another one, probably its partner, had got caught in the witch grass patch, and the witch grass was engulfing it. The survived partner was sadly looking at its partner caught into the witch grass.

Seeing this, Parjanya and Vasudha bothwere shocked.At the same time there was a commotion among the cows and buffaloes as well, they were little far away though. But there was some sharp witchy noise from patches of that direction as well.

Immediately Parjanya and Vasudha ran towards that direction then. However nothing was there, but as if it was just daunting act from the witch grass, so it was making such noise.

"It is encircling us, patches are spreading, growing and getting closer to one another" said Vasudha seeing some patches on that side also.

"We need to do something about this and that too on urgent basis Parjanya, please, we need to do something" Vasudha almost cried saying this.

Parjanya held her in his arms and said "Yes we need to do something really urgently, this is really dangerous" and added "Don't worry things will be alright". Parjanya kept Vasudha in her arms and looked at the sky, and thus, he could successfully hid his tears from Vasudha. He knew that the situation was becoming more dangerous day by day. And if any effective way out wasn't found out, it was sure that there will be havoc.

Parjanya softly freed Vasudha from his arms and held her chin and again said "It is just as your grandfather says, 'Mother Nature would surely give us help and till then we have to work for that'" He softly wiped off tears from Vasudha's face and they again went to the Cattle that were grazing on the far other side.

People working at farming and other cultivation fields too were frightened all the time. It was like some dark cloud had overshadowed the whole village and villagers. Now if they would see any new weed plants and grass, they would doubt it with fear and suspicion.

The animals were also under constant uneasiness. And looking to, and observing the behaviour of the elders, the children too were not feeling free, joyful and playful. Prior, the children used to play along the fields and farms when their parents would be working around. They would even help their parents and others in field work when they were asked to keep away from them. It had always been a pleasant atmosphere and time for both parents and children at farms and fields.

Saral and Mohan were at the medicinal plantations today. Velu and Buma were the two experts in the medicines. Proper plain land was very scarce in this hilly region and now the witch grass had started grabbing cultivable and useful land, and that was the concern of the villagers.

"This witch grass must be stopped progressing anyhow, see, yesterday it was up to that boulder and today it has come little closer Velula" Mohan said worriedly.

"You are right Mohan, we need to stop it somehow and Mother Nature will help us in that but till then we need to continue our work with faith. I have planted some vital intoxicating medicinal seeds in the border area here, let's see if it works" Velula said so much calmly that Mohan and Saral looked to each other and understood what it must be taking to be a perfect *Walaha*.

At the lunch time all the women had arrived to the fields with food stuffs for their men working there. Prior they sometimes used to bring their kids along with their study materials and would spend rest of the day time there teaching their kids new things and helping their men in the fields. But now they all were in some sort of hurry of going back home early as their kids were alone at home.

At the evening time Parjanya was getting back to village along with all the cows and other livestock he had taken out to graze. He had counted all of them, and now as every time, he was leading them to village. On his way back to village, he met Velula, Mohan and Saral, who also were returning home after finishing their work for today.

"Why are you holding this grass bunch Parjanya? Aren't they eating well out there?" Velula asked Parjanya seeing him carrying a small bunch of grass in his one hand.
"Velula it is actually for my use, with the help of this I want to explain my great great grandfather about the witch grass threat. As we all know he is the only man alive in the village who can have some idea about this witch grass way out and I need to work upon that" said Parjanya, as if he too was having doubts about if it would work.

And that night after feeding Shivala, Parjanya made him sit for a little longer time. He lightened four earthen lamps to create more light in Shivala's room. Then he held that grass bunch in his one hand and he very gently with love held Shivala's face in his other hand, and to his immense surprise, Shivala was looking straight to him only. Parjanya felt happy about it, as most of the times Shivala would look into blank only.

"Shivala, I am Parjanya, I know you know me. You know everything, because you are Shivala! We all are in a very difficult and treacherous situation. And only you can save us all from this" saying this with so much emotions in his voice, Parjanya then started waving that grass in front of Shivala's eyes, he kept doing it on and on. He was looking at Shivala with great expectation. After some time, he sat in front of him and put the grass on floor in a manner that the grass on the floor looked like as if grown there, and then he started waving it there even, he made some sound that witch grass had been making. But alas! Shivala had again started looking into the blank.

"Shivala.. please look at here.. please Shivala.. This.. this demon is engulfing our *Parubhumi* Shivala.. Please help us.. We all are going to die if we can't stop the witch grass in time. We need your help Shivala.. Help us please.."Parjanya pleaded hard, he was getting highly disappointed at the same time, realising Shivala as always, was just like a statue.

Parjanya kept waving that grass in different styles till he realised that his great great grandfather wasn't looking at all at that anymore and had fallen asleep in fact. Parjanya kept waving the grass bundles with both hands quickly as if he had gone mad. He continued it with sobbing in pain and finally he broke down and he went out of the room with his eyes full of tears.

CHAPTER ELEVEN

"I never have seen this happening in my entire life, that's all I can say. But on the other hand, what point Parjanya has made is also important and critical as well" Neharla told to the men gathered at the Holy Stones field.

Again Pattika was called on. And especially all the seven *Walaha*s and Jhanula were asked to remain present there.

Parjanya had been with the cattle for the maximum period throughout his life. Parjanya had expressed his concerns about fodder grass shortage in upcoming days due to the spread of the witch grass and its engulfing the cultivable land gradually. He had observed precisely that the witch grass patches were spreading and merging with one another day by day. And after some days, it won't be possible even to cross them by walking through them. And then the entire village would be encircled by the witch grass. Though everybody knew that the village was getting surrounded but except Parjanya no one else could foresee the possible crisis of cattle fodder. One evening Parjanya, after returning from the cattle duty, straight went to Vasudha's home to meet Neharla to express his concerns.

Immediately Neharla got an overview and could predict the possible grim situation that would arise after some days. And hence he called on this gathering at the Holy Stones field.

"I too have never ever heard of such thing that *Walahas* had gone outside the village for more than once in a year" said Hanula.

"But at the same time what Parjanya has pointed out is also important and serious thing as well, we need to address it before it is too late. So I would request Neharla, our leader, and the Pattika to take some decision in this matter" Hanula finished and sat again.

"In fact we need to act more urgently than we could think, as this witch grass soon will encircle us completely and then we won't be able to go out" Kadrula said.

"But how long that grass and cattle feed would last? How much the *Walahas* can carry? I mean seven of us. That much quantity would also get depleted one day and then what? We might have been surrounded by the witch grass by that time" said Hajala, one of the *Walahas*, who very rarely would express his thoughts.

However Bhola and other few supported that, more or less they all were of the same opinion that it was better to have something than nothing.

"Then we should immediately send our *Walahas* to fetch grass and other necessary things to sustain the cattle and other lives. How long we will be able to sustain is another thing, but who knows, by then Mother Nature may give her help and save us, save this *Parubhumi*. What is in our hands and what we can do, we should do" Neharla said.

"I would request Hanula to prepare for *Parama* omen ritual from Mother Nature with Holy *Valli*. Let's see what Mother of all of us wants us to do" he further said.

"So all the *Walahas* please get ready by afternoon, let's hope that Mother Nature would guide us and bless us in our efforts for survival" saying this Neharla stood up and so did all the other men there.

"So you are going again" Vasudha said while putting a morsel in Parjanya's mouth. Vasudha had brought lunch for Parjanya that day when she came to know about *Walahas*' leaving again.

"Yes and would go in search of some rare and important plants and medicinal fruits along with the grass for cattle, as Kadrula told us all after the gathering" Parjanya replied putting a colic in Vasudha's mouth now.

"Since we are not going only for cattle food but for other plants and medicinal fruits too, which can be found in the far surroundings, we will have to go farthest this time" Parjanya added.

"And when will you be back this time?" Vasudha asked anxiously as if wanted to hear something that was on her mind already.

"As per what Kadrula told to all the *Walahas*, it can't be fixed, as it depends more on how early we find the other required things from the jungle. As the Pattika has asked to assess the cattle feed requirement and other necessary things too" said Parjanya.

"Parjanya, will we be able to defeat and control this witch grass?" Vasudha asked as if controlling her tears.

"Yes Vasudha, we will for sure, Neharla said, Mother Nature has always helped *Parubhumi* with her blessings and this time too she will bless us. But meanwhile, you continue doing what I have taught you just now, okay? Grass is there at home. It is important that Shivala understands it, and if he does, we will definitely have our way out" said Parjanya looking into Vasudha's eyes, which were hopeful but fearful at the same time!

At the evening time, Parjanya as always was coming back with the cattle from the grazing fields. He had carefully got all the cattles passed through the small patches around and as always he was walking at the end. He was very much in thoughts while walking as well. And suddenly he heard some uproar ahead of him where all the cattles were going to. He ran faster and reached there. It was Salaka, one cow, who had laid on the ground and was breathing fast and heavily as if not been able to breathe properly. Couple of men and women had gathered there. They were just passing from there; they stopped seeing the cow in that situation. "I have seen that she had just drunk water from this *nira* and immediately fallen down" Maaraali, wife of Mohan told Parjanya. It was difficult for Parjanya to believe that but in a fraction of second he could make it. He ran by the side of that particular *nira* upto its entry point and immediately put the wooden barricade to stop more water coming there. By that time Kala, Govind and other men had arrived there. Govind ran to inform and call Jhanula.

"She will be fine in couple of days" Jhanula said. All were at the *Gaughar*. Neharla and Kadrula were upset. Everyone else too were very much tensed.

"I had gone to the original stream of that particular *nira*, and as expected, I found the witch grass touching the water flowing from that *nira*" Parjanya informed everyone there with real worry.

"I should have anticipated this after the emergence of the witch grass" Virajla at once admitted his big lapse.

"Nevermind Viraj, our Salaka would be alright and now we know that the witch grass can even spread its poisonous evil effect by contaminating water as well" Kadrula said with a deep sigh.

"One thing I have noticed, as this is my daily and regular route of bringing all the cattles back, the witch grass was not present there in that area few days back only, but it has started emerging there, after Virajla had made *nira* there" Parjanya said.

And Neharla looked up, "We all will have to be very careful Kadru, very careful. This witch grass is more dangerous than what I thought of" he said.

Paataali along with other women came there and said "Let's make few *Tundus* in the mainland village area. We can not rely on streams now. We have to store water for longer time consumption, as once the witch grass surrounds and confines us completely; we should have enough supply of water with us. Hence we, the village women, would start bringing water from the main streams itself from tomorrow".

"Yes we should start making *Tundus* on urgent basis, Paataali is right, we had missed this important point regarding necessity of water" Kadrula said.

The Pattika was impressed with the women for bringing such important point to their notice and also for suggesting the way out.

"Okay, let's start making the *Tundus* right from tomorrow morning after the *Walahas* leave for the trip" Neharla said.

Jhanula looked at Kadrula and in a slight eye contact, he coveyed Kadrula something.

Jhanula and Kadrula met late that night. "Kadrula, I need some very important and useful varieties of plants and fruits from this trip. What I can see about our future is really serious. I couldn't disclose there among the Pattika about its seriousness but believe me we all are going to be in real bleak situation in coming days" he said.

"I too know that Jhanu, but all we can do now is trust Mother Nature, and trust ourselves, keep fighting against the enemy" saying this Kadrula put his hand on Jhanula's shoulder. It was like both were trying to console eachother for something they first would convince themselves for!

Keeping in mind the possible ill effects of witch grass on humans as well as animals, Jhanula asked Kadrula to bring certain Himalayan medicinal plants and fruits which were rare to find but they were vital for their sustenance now on. Jhanula had depicted each small detail of every needed medicinal palnt and fruit required. And Kadrula was getting even more confused with depictions of each next variety from Jhanula. It was necessary for Jhanula to remain present in the village in order to be helpful in any medical emergency to any human or animal, else he would have proposed for permission to go with *Walaha*s to bring all the medicinal plants and fruits he needed. Finally, when Kadrul left from Jhanula's home, he was crammed with details in terms of shape, smell and colours of different varieties of medicinal plants and fruits. He was pretty tensed to memorise all that and just to get some respite he breathed-in big and look up the sky, but he felt as if the moon was laughing at him!

Hanula was chanting the holy hymns turning towards all the four directions, holding the holy water pot in his hands and sprinkling it to all four directions at the same time. The Holy *Valli* was as always kept open and placed at the centre stone of the Holy Stones field.

All the seven *Walaha*s were ready in their traditional outfit and with those special wooden sticks on their right shoulders.

In the front and foremost was Kadrula, the senior most *Walaha*, steady as rock, as always. Parjanya was in the last position. All the *Walaha*s were having different feeling this time in their hearts which could be seen on their faces as well. This was first ever time that they were going out of village for more than once in the same year. And this time it was regarding survival against the threat from the evil. But as always people of *Parubhumi* were hopeful and had faith in the almighty, the Mother Nature. They had been like this for centuries.

Kadrula was performing all the rituals as directed by Hanula, and so the other *Walahas* too, but even the most experienced Kadrula wasn't able to hide his stress of doing something unusual. Being *Walaha* was considered to be the most prestigious status but at the same time, they always have to follow and go by all the rules of Mother Nature very strictly. Failing to any of which deliberately or by mistake would bring peril to him, his family and the village as a whole invariably. And there were such examples in past too.

There wasn't that ice bridge anymore on the valley of roots. So that was to be decided from the Holy *Valli*. And as per the Holy *Valli* indication, to the direction of a bird call, the *Walahas* were to leave from that direction only. After a while a bird call was heard from the east side. It was exactly close to the valley of vihar and all the *Walahas* stepped down it one by one after the village pujari Hanula finally permitted them to leave.

Almost all the villagers were there. Women of the *Walahas* were much concerned and tensed in particular. They all kept seeing them going away and away. And after they finally disappeared behind the small mountains, all the villagers did get back to the village.

But Vasudha remained there; she found that even the birds were not chirping delightfully. There was a heavy stillness in place of that pure mountain stillness. And suddenly someone from behind put a hand on her shoulder, Vasudha got startled at once and looked back, it was Mahi.

"He will come back safely do not worry Vasudha" saying that Mahi sat beside Vasudha.

"Yeah he will, I know, but he had to venture this expedition solely due to this enigma, and he had to go because of this" Vasudha said pointing one of the witch grass patches nereby.

Had there been usual days and conditions, Vasudha would have verily asked Mahi to pay a visit to Umi Uni valleys for her birds or the streams and they both would have had congenial time together along with other friends.

But nowadays every villager was not living the way he or she used to live prior the witch grass threat. They knew that they are under a grave menace. All the homemakers and women were melancholic and worried round the clock. Women of Parubhumi were not only the homemakers; they were equally having their leisure time together. Singing, dancing and playing various games by forming groups was their unique style to relax.

They would impart their skills of copious crafts to young girls of village through the course of leisure time comprising of indispensable adroitness to sustain and develop.

Both Vasudha and Mahi perched quietly there overlong; the sun was preparing to set. It had been onerous for Vasudha when Parjanya first went out of village as *Walaha*. And this time too, it had been only minutes since Parjanya had left and Vasudha had started yearning for him!

Finally, they got up and started walking back towards the village with the same faith and hope in their hearts that the rising Sun tomorrow would come up with the day when they all would be able to defeat and remove that demon from their land.

CHAPTER TWELVE

"No... No... You can't do this, you can't do this Shivala, please don't do this" Vasudha broke into tears.

Mahi and Dwija held her by her arms and made her stand on her feet.

For the last two days Vasudha was giving a try to make Shivala realise and see the grass which she would hold in her hands as taught by Parjanya. She had done everything to make Shivala feel something with the grass but there was no result on Shivala. All the three girls were highly disappointed. Not only because Parjanya had asked Vasudha to give try about Shivala but all the villagers were also hoping and talking of that only, if Shivala can help and for that Shivala had to see or realise the grass first in order to recall something about past. Few women literally had gathered outside Parjanya's home where Vasudha was trying to work on Shivala but they too secretly left dejected seeing Vasudha broken down.

Not only of the grass, Shivala didn't have any effect of tears and pain of a young girl too, who was crying in colossal pain. Mahi laid down Shivala on his bed. Shivala was still looking in the blank; she wiped off her own tears and then came out to Vasudha.

Vasudha got broken down because she and all the villagers knew that the witch grass patches were increasing in size and shape, even the *Walahas* who had gone out for grass and cattle feed, would have to enter the village very carefully negotiating the grass patches as they had grown bigger and covered more land than ever before.

It was like the witch grass was attempting to block the entry point of the *Walahas*!

Now it had been observed that the witch grass can even engulf the sunlight and there was only little light on the grass patches even under the full Sun. The witch grass would engulf everything and would not set free anything that would get into its hold.

The increasing patches were increasing worries for the villagers as well. People associated with the cattle grazing job had to be quite watchful as there were very narrow paths on which the animals had to walk to and fro and moreover, the most experienced man for this job was out of the village these days.

Neharla had appointed few young men just to keep an eye on the daily and in fact momentarily activities in terms of sudden increase of witch grass. Because of the constant and accurate vigil, it was discovered that the witch grass augmented in the night time than the day light. It was also established that people staying close to the witch grass for longer time were seen fallen into depression due to ill effect of the witch grass. Such people would act sluggish as they don't want to do anything anymore. The witch grass was life sucking indeed.

The witch grass had such power to suck life and liveliness from everything. All the birds and the animals, pet animals too were substantially affected by its life sucking power.

Just as last two days, Vasudha returned home with disappointment. She entered and straight away went to her room.

But today Paataali could see that Vasudha had cried too much. Paataali went to Vasudha who was sitting at a favorite window of her room and as always gazing the sky with tears still knocking her eyes.

"Sometimes destiny doesn't wish to grant us or even share with us any credit of something great" saying this Paataali held chin of her only beloved daughter and made her look at her.

There were tears in the eyes of Vasudha. She kept looking at her mother who was her ideal for countless things in her life. She always had admired the fortitude of her mother.

"Mother Nature has her ways for everything, my child. This witch grass too is not something out of her lap. She exclusively creates and destroys. We are all part and particles of Mother Nature, you, I and that witch grass and everything else."

"Come, get up and get fresh, I have made milk with sweet mints, your favourite, and Parjanya's too, he is coming back today" Paataali pulled Vasudha up and made her stand.

Vasudha got up and hugged her mother tight. Paataali kept caressing on her back.

"Kadrula please share your half burden with me. I can still bear much more than what I am carrying" Parjanya said.

Parjanya was the sixth person to offer this help to Kadrula after the first five senior *Walahas*.
All the *Walahas* were on their way back to home. All they had gone for was grass for cattle feed and other rare medicinal fruits and plants, and all they were carrying, was that only. Each of them was overloaded with the huge hays. As Kadrula, the leader *Walaha*, was the eldest among them, all the other *Walahas* had offered assistance to him to share from his load. But Kadrula was

a staunch oldie. He was carrying the equal portion of grass hays along with the other *Walahas*.

They had spent their first two days merely in cutting and stocking the fodder grass which was in abundance out there and today on the third day, from morning to noon they had fastened hay stacks carefully in a manner that they could be carried comfortably with optimum load. Meanwhile Kadrula had left for little farther and in the more dense parts of woods early in the morning itself. He instructed all the other *Walahas* to prepare things and be equipped. Once Kadrula left, all the *Walahas* talked with one another about Kadrula's going alone and its noteworthiness and urgency as well. They surmised it to be some medicinal fruits and plants Kadrula must have aimed for. All of them earnestly prayed Mother Nature to bestow Kadrula in acquiring those things which ultimately were going to succor Parubhumi. Kadrula came back in the afternoon carrying plentiful different stuff. He utterly asked about the preparations and told rest of them that he would spill the beans about his secret visit at the right time. After every strand of grass was carefully bound and tied up, as part of ritual, Kadrula chanted specific indebtedness hymns for Mother Nature and proceeded for home.

As they had calculated, the fodder grass they accumulated was to last utmost for a week as per Parjanya, as he was a proficient person as far as cattle grazing was concerned. So every *Walaha* was apprehensive for the upcoming time, after one week.

However Kadrula had told them that Jhanula, the village chief Vaidya, had suggested some herbs to bring without fail which were to be used on this grass prior feeding the cattle. And with that herbal liquid, the cattle would not only find it stuffed heavily but also they will be getting vital nourishing and nutritional elements from it, also the herbal liquid was to help in increasing the milk production as well as keeping all the animals healthy.

But yet, each *Walaha*, while leaving and crossing the pasture, were distinctively having the same one idea on their mind, and that was, let me pluck some more grass!

As decided, the village pujari Hanula along with Neharla and few more men were waiting at the vihar valley, from where the *Walaha*s were to enter the village. It was evening by now. Everyone was keen to see how much fodder grass the *Walaha*s were bringing with them. And after sometime, they were spotted, far at distance. In fact the *Walaha*s were not visible at all, as they were covered by bulky stacks of grass. But the first haystack was sighted, a gigantic boulder like haystack was that, followed by the same other giant piles one by one. They were heading from the west with the setting sun. Everyone at the village was exhilarated. Since centuries, *Walaha*s would go out of village only once in a year and that was not followed this year, hence Neharla and Hanula both were not at ease, because the *Walaha*s were yet to cross the entry bridge which was man-made now, with big tree trunks; and they both were the witness of what had happened in the past. All the *Walaha*s, after successfully crossing all the cliffs and rifts, eventually arrived exactly after an hour.

First was Kadrula, the stalwart leader, followed by Bhola, Tatu, Haja, Buma, Velu and lastly Parjanya.

The real task now was to traverse the valley of vihar, as the *Walaha*s now had to cross it with the haystacks they were carrying. Unlike the valley of roots, the valley of vihaar was steeper. Kadrula was so energetic as if he just had come out of his home after having meal, called all the other *Walaha*s close by and talked to them. All the other *Walaha*s seemed to understand the trick Kadrula had taught them. All of them formed the line standing in the reverse position and started climbing in the reverse order! The trick worked, the *Walaha*s conveniently entered the village premises after crossing the Valley of Vihar then. Miraculously the witch grass couldn't grow as briskly here as it had on the other parts. All the *Walaha*s then took place in a fixed formation in a circle. Hanula started chanting the holy Mantras. At the same time, he was sprinkling the holy water on all *Walaha*s. Hanula took back the *Meta* sticks from each *Walaha* at the time of ritual. Soon after that, he hinted with his hand's gesture, to show that *Walaha*s could now enter the village and only after that the *Walaha*s stepped on the village land.

As soon as they entered, they all subsequently put down the haystacks they were carrying up to now. There was joviality among the people congregated there. The other young men of the village were readily waiting to carry away the grass brought by the *Walaha*s. They picked up the grass haystacks and landed it to the village *Bhandaras* where it was to be safeguarded and distributed to the cattle on daily basis as per requirement and as directed by Jhanula.

Neharla thanked all the *Walaha*s for their paramount aid. He and Jhanula at once asked Kadrula for the rare and vital medicinal plants and fruits they asked to bring with. It was something very crucial because that would enable the village to fight well for longer time against the witch grass. Neharla expressed his gratitude to Parjanya separately, as he was the person who had foreseen this pivotal issue very timely. Parjanya was overwhelmed that he just smiled and got shy. He was in a hell lot of hurry to leave that place, as the two persons he loved the most were there in the village, one of them must be waiting for him to come back since the day he left, he was sure about that.

"But what after one week? though grandpa was saying that Jhanula has formulated a herbal liquid which will be advantageous for cattle in many ways still.." Vasudha could not say anything further.

"And how about the witch grass, is it still spreading rapidly? Parjanya curiously asked.

"Yes it is spreading steadily; it is spreading every minute daily. Everyday new patches are emerging and the older ones too are extending. The grass is getting taller as well. And you know what, it has now started making that witchy sound too often, especially at night" Vasudha said in sinking voice.

Parjanya at once got up. It was night already.

"Come, let's see" he said. Vasudha was flabbergasted but she didn't stop Parjanya.

And both went to the witch grass to see and experience the witchy sound that Vasudha was telling about.

Vasudha led Parjanya to one of the most grown up patches area of the village surroundings. It was pitch dark at the valley of roots and pretty cold wind was blowing. And with that wind, the witch grass was producing its infamous witchy sound Tchi.... Tchi..... Tchi....

Both, Parjanya and Vasudha were speechless. Parjanya held Vasudha's hand and made her sit beside him on to the nearby boulder. They could see that a few patches were actually now taller than a sheep's height.

"Any sign from Shivala?" after a prolonged silence, Parjanya broke the silence.

"No, nothing" she hardly could speak.

And at that very moment, the biggest patch of witch grass, as if laughing in audacity, started its cacophony. Tchi.... Tchi.... Tchi....

Vasudha could sense a sigh from Parjanya in that discordant witch sound too.

CHAPTER THIRTEEN

Tchi.... Tchi... Tchi... The same witchy noise!

And everyone standing there in front of it was in a deep anguish.

That was another attempt to make Shivala perceive something about the witch grass. Shivala was once again brought to the witch grass on the insistence of Parjanya. He was desperate now.

The witch grass was now lofty and was proliferating almost everywhere around the village. Earlier there were witch grass patches and now there were few patches of some open land left around the village!

And though the witch grass was making a very sharp unpleasant noise, Shivala had no impact on it. As always, he was staring in blank only, with the same emotionless and indifferent face.

Few men corralled there receded for their designated job as they lost hopes on Shivala. This was the time of farming and land cultivation for grain, medicine and fruits. Hence Neharla asked them not to squander the time and continue with their daily work. That experienced man knew very well that people, if left with no work, they certainly would be hopeless and would fall into depression.

However, it was almost sure that if the witch grass was not controlled or destroyed sooner, it would gulp and kill everything slowly and steadily by beneathing the land.

Yet again there was a strong determination on Parjanya's face today. He had proposed that Shivala should be brought to the witch grass one more time. Parjanya was sitting just beside his great great grandfather on his wooden bed only. Both Shivala and Parjanya were silent. Both of them were unmoved. Both were looking in the same direction and same object as well. Only difference was, there was a deadpan in one man's eyes and conviction in other's.

Couple of more hours passed by, Shivala was already asleep as he always would do. But Parjanya still was sitting right there quietly.

At noon, Neharla again asked Parjanya to take Shivala back and Parjanya again respectfully denied the same. So both Neharla and Kadrula left from the Uni Umi valley where Shivala was placed today.

So now Parjanya was alone with Shivala there. Parjanya was still looking at the tallest and widest witch grass patch there. He was in cavernous dismay.

Parubhumi was the most sacred land on this earth he believed. It was his home. He was born there, grown up there. And now the same home was under a threat and jeopardy. And if that threat is not addressed well-timed, it would surely destroy everything. Parjanya again started feeling guilty for he brought flowers and fruits surreptitiously for Vasudha. This entire hazard might well be because of that too, he was contemplating.

And suddenly one hand touched his shoulders from behind. Parjanya startled a bit and turned back. Vasudha was there. She was looking undeviating into Parjanya's wet eyes. And for the first time ever in life, Parjanya rolled his eyes away from Vasudha's eyes. He was indeed disheartened. Vasudha sat by him and took one of his hands in her hands.

"You know Parjanya, when you were out for getting cattle grass and I was struggling to make Shivala see and realise something about the witch grass, once I got disappointed and cried a lot. And that day, my mother apprised me that sometimes the destiny doesn't wish that we get credit for something great or she doesn't wish even to share the credit. She would do it on her own and bless us, just. My mom also added that there is nothing in this universe which has not come from the lap of Mother Nature. And as everything, this witch grass is one of the creations of Mother Nature so she would unquestionably do something about it too".

Parjanya listened to it looking still at the witch grass patch which was making that tchi tchi tchi sound in between.

After sometime, Vasudha took out the food and offered lunch but Parjanya denied. Vasudha persuaded Parjanya a lot with all her heart but Parjanya with all his love denied it completely.

Vasudha put back all the stuff and packed it again. They both sat for couple of hours silently and vacantly towards the witch grass. Both of them had lots of memories of their childhood about this very place where they were sitting right now.

Shivala woke up once again. They helped him sit. Shivala was to be given hot milk with that herb root at the dinner time only, as most of the time in a day he just would sleep sleep and sleep merely.

Parjanya again attempted to make Shivala discern something about the witch grass. He continued it till Shivala again fallen into sleep and then he again got gloomy.

It was evening now, so Vasudha asked Parjanya to get back to home along with Shivala. But to her immense surprise, Parjanya informed Vasudha that he was going to stay there for entire night with Shivala.

Vasudha was short of words but she knew that Parjanya was taking this pain to find a way or solution for this menace. So she didn't try to deny the idea and she finally left.
"No, I am not going to leave from here, please this is important Neharla. Please let me try, who knows if Shivala could perceive something about the witch grass only in the night time?" said Parjanya with great amount of optimism.

"Okay, but you alone can't stay here like this. Apart from the witch grass, there is a predators' threat as well. So Govind and Saral would also accompany you" said

Neharla, looking at Govind and Saral.

They both showed their readiness at once.

Parjanya tried to oppose that, but Kadrula too forced him for that, so he finally had to give in.

After late evening, the three of them had their meal and tucked themselves in the blankets brought by Saral, as the cold winds had started blowing.

Shivala too was fed with milk mixed with herbs and roots as his only daily meal course. And once again Parjanya Saral and Govind tried their best to make Shivala to realize about the witch grass. They brought Shivala so much closer to the bigger patch there which was making the loudest tchi tchi tchi sound. Three of them could hardly bear and stand there. It was really causing a great pain. But Shivala had no effect on him whatsoever. He was just looking into the blank with unmoving eyes.

Finally, he was brought back to his wooden bed and he fell asleep again. All three of them knew that the witch grass was making slow progress inch by inch without being noticed and making the tchi.. tchi.. tchi.. sound loudly.

CHAPTER FOURTEEN

Everyone who was on a stroll in the morning was looking at Parjanya with great sympathy and respect at the same time. However, Parjanya, along with Saral Govind and Kala, was walking with his head down. They were taking Shival back home in the early morning.

Kala had joined them in the night itself. Kala had brought extra beddings and warm clothes for all the three there. And he too put in all the efforts to sensitize Shivala about the witch grass along with Parjanya Saral and Govind, but Shivala was just as always, blank. While bringing Shivala back to home, Kala was crying for the unsuccessful night they had.

The onlookers were heartbroken too. As all knew that the witch grass, that has started spreading a little more quickly, was a fatal threat. And only possible solution could come through Shivala. And the down headed Parjanya could well express how the night was.

The three-night partners of Parjanya sat there after landing Shivala safely in his room. Parjanya thanked them all but they were in fact deeply touched by Parjanya's endeavor to save the village. Kala again flowed with emotions and hugged Parjanya. Parjanya consoled him and then all the three left from there.

Parjanya started cooking food for him, as he was to go for the cattle grazing duty today. He knew that witch grass patches were burgeoning and hence with massive care he had to guide the animals through those patches. Though the animals too were heedful but any mistake could cost life of an innocent animal.

Parjanya after having his breakfast reached the *Gaushala*. As always, he released the cattle first. Parjanya was to be accompanied by Adhu and Buka today. Because of witch grass, each animal had to be handled carefully through the patches to reach to the pastures. And now the animals too sometimes be so fearful that they become reluctant to move close to the witch grass. So it was a challenge to through all the animals to the grazing field. It was more the hunger urge of the animals that would force them to pass through the witch grass and reach to the lea. However, the open grasslands too were shrinking and diminishing. But when Parjanya reached to the regular grazing ground at *Busa* Mountain in west, he saw that it was not possible to through the animals now without being touched and got caught by the witch grass. Parjanya, Buka and Adhu were disenchanted. They decided to examine the patches properly and they finally concluded not to take the risk. They took all the animals back from that site and headed southwards taking a round passing the valley of roots. And that very place reminded Parjanya of Vasudha, he blushed a bit and kept walking.

Now they were at the North grazing grounds where it was even more adjoining patches. They found that the animals too were exhausted as they had walked a long distance today.

"We can't take risk here too" Parjanya said.

"Yeah here patches are even closer, now what?" asked Adhu.

"Let's take them back to the *Gaushala*" said Parjanya.

And after stretching out for some time, they started their journey back to the village *Gaushala.*
While entering the village they met Bhola. He exclaimed about coming back early from the grazing. Parjanya informed Bhola about the situation at pastures.

All the animals were settled back in the shed. Neharla was intimated and meanwhile the news became hot potato in the village. Jhanula, the village *Vaidya*, was called on. He of course had kept the herbal liquid ready to use whenever required. So the fodder grass warehouse had to be unlocked earlier than expected.

Necessary estimated grass was taken out from it. Jhanula scrupulously sprayed the herbal liquid on all grass stacks. And all the animals were fed there at the cattle shed only.

Parjanya was seeing all these and getting shattered inside. Some villagers had clustered together to watch the new way of cattle feeding today. Among them Vasudha too was there and could see tears in Parjanya's eyes even from far distance. However the animals were eating the grass with interest and gratification.

No one was speaking; almost all the men were there at the holy stones field in the evening that day yet it was hushful. They all were immensely anxious. They were, for the first time, clutched by the witch grass from each direction.

And this time it was not a planned gathering or called on gathering as well. In reality all the villagers were much frightened that they felt it safer keeping themselves close to one another.

Even Neharla and Kadrula - the two senior most and strong personalities too were finding it grueling whether they should motivate the villagers to maintain hopes, and if they should, how?

"We should at least let the cattle out of the sheds daily for twice, as they are habituated to that" Parjanya said, as if trying to keep the fear at bay by breaking the silence.

"Yes correct, let them roam freely at least for couple of times in a day" Virajla supported it. That man knew that it was imperative to keep people's hopes and moral up during this testing time.

"This witch grass has started growing and spreading little quicker than earlier I think" Parjanya said with a deep sigh.

"I have detected the cause behind it" Jhanula said.

Everybody looked at him with all ears.

"We are in the waning moon cycle these days. This witch grass grows quickly in the dark. Few days back it was a waxing moon cycle but now it is waning time and moon is almost not there throughout the night, so the grass is growing rapidly." Jhanula put two and two together.

"Then how many days we are left with till the witch grass arrives at the village?" Kadrula asked.

"I suppose we may have round about 10 days, as the half of the darkdays have passed". After that there will be a waxing moon again which would slow down the growth and progress of the witch grass" Jhanula said.

"Shall we not again go out and stock more grass and food for the animals?" Parjanya asked looking in the blank. "I don't think that would be useful good deal." Kadrula said with a deep sigh and continued, "If this witch grass keeps engulfing everything like this, the chances of survival are less after a while. None of us will be alive gradually" he added.

All present there drowned in the deep distress and sadness. No one was broaching and it was again the mortal silence.

"Let us all move out from *Parubhumi* before it is too late" Haja said.

"No" Neharla intervened.

"But why, why can't we move and leave this place?" Bhola, Tatu, Saral and couple of other men asked almost together. They all were getting frustrated now.

"I don't know what to do to destroy or control this witch grass, but all I know is we can't, we just can't leave Parubhumi ever Tatu, never we can leave this place" said Neharla.

And after couple of moments, he gathered himself and looked up and said,

"Okay, Now I am splitting a secret that I have inherited from my father. My father might have heard this from his father and my grandfather from his father. It is said that many years ago there came a man here. He was a lonely wanderer Saint and he had the exceptional power to listen and talk to lands and mountains, valleys and trees. In a way he could talk and listen to everything of Nature. That Saint knew every inch of this great Himalayas where our *Parubhumi* is situated. One day while passing from this particular land, he heard the sobbing and callings from this part of land. So he paused and tried talking back. In that conversation he came to know that, this land, *Paubhumi* what we call it now, was unhappy because no human being or animals and birds were living here on its land, as it was a cursed land. That Saint offered solace to the land and countered that there was neither water nor vegetation around and the Land itself was rock hard that no one would be able to cultivate that for sustenance. In response to that, the land promised all those luxury and necessities once the living objects start settling and living there. And after hearing this, that great Saint gave a word to this land that he would do his best to eradicate its curse. The Land then became joyous and offered every possible blessing but it had one condition stating that anyone once dwelled here and born here, could never ever move out and leave this land; they have to live here till life.

That great Saint had vowed the same to this land. He then managed to live there and also moved his successors on this land. Gradually, centuries after, this village came into existence and emerged as *Parubhumi*.

It was the mutual agreement between this land and that great Saint. Hence if anyone dares to breach that accord, he or she along with this village, would suffer the wrath of this land and mountains" Neharla finished with heavy breathe. "However it was allowed to step out of village once a year to fetch the unobtainable here but necessary things for sustenance, mainly seeds and plants". Neharla further added.

Everyone present there was dumbstruck to speak anything. As if they were in a vacuum.

Kadrula too wasn't aware of this folk tale up to now. So he said "Then there is no question of stepping out. Let's just be here, just here".

"Yeah let's embrace the death tenderly, let's feel, let's feel the death softly" Mohan and Haza mocked almost together with different voice and tone.

Parjanya too was speechless after learning this.

But after couple of seconds, suddenly Parjanya got up in a spur of the moment.

Everyone there looked at him with little surprise as Parjanya was so brisk as if overflown with powering emotions. "Yes feeling it, yeah perfect, yeah feeling it, yes" and repeating all these, he started running to the village *Bhandaraas*, followed by Mohan,

Saral and Govind.

Neither Kadrula nor anyone else could conceive anything of that.

"I think he has got some clue" said Neharla.

"Yes, let's hope it works, whatever it is, it works" said Hanula.

And everyone headed for home with some sort of excitement mixed with hope.

It was the fifth day today. And today too Parjanya was carrying the same smaller size grass bundles with him from the village *Bhandaras* and taking them to his home. The village people were watching this, what Parjanya had started doing for the last four days.

For the last four days, Parjanya was filling Shivala's room with the fodder grass that the *Walahas* had brought with them from their last special expedition. Parjanya was filling the room gradually. He had suddenly got this idea when he was sitting along with other village men at the Holy Stones field. He just ran from that meeting and went straight to the village *Bhandaras*. Parjanya convinced Neharla about what he was doing, but Neharla didn't seem to have understood what exactly Parjanya was intending to do with those small bundles of grazing grass. But since Kadrula and other *Walahas* were much optimistic and there was no other way to try, every villager was excited for Parjanya's idea. But as usual, people started losing hope from Parjanya's idea too as it had been four days and it came out that Shivala hadn't looked at those grass bundles yet. And this was a strong reason for people to lose hope and faith from Parjanya's idea as for the first time entire *Parubhumi* was surrounded completely by the witch grass siege. Only couple of valley areas were out of it somehow, and no one knew the reasons for that. But those areas were of no use either for Humans or animals for anything.

However, Parjanya hadn't lost hope from his idea of grass bundles. Neither would he try to explain to people how it would work. But he knew what can make Shivala realise about the presence of witch grass. The prime argument of the village people and now even Neharla too was, why Parjanya should not fill up Shivala's room with grass bundles in one go, and why gradually? As they all were running out of time now. But Parjanya was determined about his idea's success this way only. And Kadrula was now the only person in support of Parjanya's trick of using the grass bundles gradually.

The village people had now started praying to Mother Nature regularly. The Holy Stones field was now continuously occupied by one or more villagers offering prayers to Mother Nature. Prayer was the medium of ultimate hope for the people of Parubhumi.

Hanula had started sitting for prayers almost for entire day. He would chant the holy *Shlokas* and Hymns throughout for the past few days.

He also had started the mass prayer sessions in the late evening at the Holy Stones field and each villager from a child to an old man was attending that mass prayer session.

The *Parubhumi* had its history right from the beginning, and that was based on faith and beliefs in Nature as Supreme authority. And so the people of *Parubhumi*, since ages, were grown up learning the same.

And today was the seventh day since Parjanya had started stuffing the grass in Shivala's room. So after the seventh day's mass prayer, all the villagers were very much restless especially women.

The witch grass had made considerable progress during these days. And as one of its ill effects people started feeling depressed and inert.

However Paataali was the lady who had taken up that front with adorable spirit and faith. She started engaging women in the field works more now, especially after the witch grass started growing faster. The witch grass was now not much far from the fields and farms though.

Paataali wanted the village women to see and face the witch grass in order to prepare them to fight against it, if not physically then of course mentally, with their true strong spirit.

"But why not stuffing the room of Shivala once and for all? We are really running out of time now" Bhola adamantly put up his point after the late evening prayer.

All the men and women present there backed up the same while murmuring.
"No, it is important that Shivala realises it gradually. If we commit a little haste, the whole idea can be defeated" Parjanya was very much confident somehow.

"Let Parjanya do it the way he intends to do it. He has done everything to make Shivala perceive about the witch grass. He has put in all his efforts whole heartedly but Shivala couldn't realise up to now. And this is the last hope and chance for all of us. If Shivala understands it with this trick, then we will have survival ray of hope." Kadrula said supporting Parjanya as always.

One more time people of Parubhumi went back home from the Holy Stones field with an anxiety in brain and hopes in heart.

And with cold breezes, the witch grass was, as if, laughing at them tchi....tchi..tchi...

"No.. no.. don't come please, don't come.. don't.." Vasudha was shouting fearfully.
As always, she had gone to her favorite place at valley of roots. But after the emergence of the witch grass, not only birds but even the flowers were not blooming around!

The witch grass had turned the whole atmosphere of Parubhumi into some mortal and grim place. There was the heaviness of acrimony vibes all around, the witch grass area which was now close to enter the village fields and farms, was always like a demon keeping its mouth wide open to engulf anything.

But after so many days some Deer had seen Vasudha from the valley and had started climbing up to reach to her as they were very well acquainted with her.
"No please no" Vasudha still was screaming.

But the Deer kept climbing up as they used to do this so many times before as well.
Listening to Vasudha shouting, they got hesitated and stopped for a while.
Vasudha knew that the witch grass had started growing from the verge of the valley and somehow it couldn't grow taller in that particular area. So it was more likely that the deer wouldn't be able to see that the moment they would put first step out ahead from the valley, they might get caught in to the witch grass.

So in a desperate attempt she even threw some stones at them, to drive them away. And finally by being heavily disappointed with such behavior from their loving lady, they turned back, surprised and sad.

Vasudha burst into tears with immense pain in her heart. They all were her friends and occasionally would visit her. She would talk to them and would pet them even. They used to trust

Vasudha so much that once they came to meet her even with their newly born fawns, which was really a rare phenomenon for Vasudha to witness.

But today Vasudha had to hurt them to their core to protect them actually yet she was broken down by her gesture which was actually the need of the moment.

"So finally it has reached the village borders" Parjanya said.

Parjanya along with Saral and Govind had gone to see the witch grass in the south at *Busa* Mountain. Along with the taller patches, the witch grass of small size that was sighted at first had entered the actual village area now. All the three man sunk into the hopelessness.

It had started covering the cultivated fields and farms now. The people of *Parubhumi* had to see witch grass engulfing their beloved and well preserved fields which were ploughed in fact in recent past.

Was this the beginning of an End?!

The same question was there on everyone's mind that time.

Three of them carefully examined and observed the entire area and then moved back towards the village.

All three sat at Parjanya's home muted. There was nothing much to say anyway. In a while, Mohan and Kala too arrived there from the valley of *vihaar*, and with the same disappointing news as well.

So now *Parubhumi* was even more closely confined by the witch grass from all sides, Parjanya was pondering.

Last night only he had stuffed few more bunches around Shivala in a manner that now Shival's wooden bed was not visible, so he could feel the grass when he happen to touch it on his own, as Shivala sometimes used to sit on his bed on his own. He had fed Shivala last night and then arranged the grass hays in a way, he thought it would be effective enough to make Shivala realise the grass, feel the grass.

And because of more use of the grass there, the cattle and animals were given only half of their daily requirement of grass these days. Though the animals too were now not eating much mostly due to lack of appetite, however Parjanya was feeling strongly that they too were supporting his cause that way!

He was dewy-eyed thinking that he hadn't been in the room of Shivala since morning.
He had done everything he could, Parjanya was celebrating endlessly. Why Mother Nature was not listening to everyone's prayers, why?

There was a cumbersome and deadly silence all over.

And suddenly Kala shouted...

"S h i v a l a................"

All of them looked up like a shot and none of them could believe what they saw!

Yes, it was Shivala!

Shivala himself came out of his room, putting his hands one by one on the room wooden walls close to him. He was covered much with grass straws.

All galloped to him. Shivala still was looking in the blank though. But it seemed that he had toiled hard to come out.

But Parjanya comprehended that, Shivala was crawling as if he was searching for something. To touch something!

His lips were quivering as if he wanted to say something but he just wasn't able to.
And he was turning around every now and again like he was looking for something.
"Hurryyyy... go...call Neharla...." Parjanya told Mohan loudly in the highest excitement.
Both, Mohan and Kala sprinted to fetch Neharla.

CHAPTER SIXTEEN

It had been almost an hour now. The whole village was congregated at Parjanya's home. Shivala with all the difficulties in moving himself was still moving here and there inch by inch very slowly. It was more of a crawling! He was constantly trying to speak and say something but was unable to.

While moving slowly he was frequently getting struck with the walls as well as pillars around. Neharla was moving step by step with Shivala. He constantly was saying "Shivala Shivala I am Nehar, your Nehar, tell me please, tell us what to do? What do you want to say? What are you looking for?"

But all that didn't seem to be working. Shivala was not stopping moving either.

For couple of times Kadrula and Neharla tried to hold Shivala's hand in order to help him walk better. But that was not accepted by Shivala it seemed, he stopped moving for a while in response to that.

So Parjanya requested Neharla and Kadrula to sit back and wait and watch for some time.

Half an hour passed by, but Shivala was still moving in the same area by taking support of the walls and pillars of his room.

"We must get clue from Shivala before he faints or go to sleep again. And we are really proud of you Parjanya. Your trick has worked finally. Though we all had doubts but yes your trick has worked great" said Neharla.

"It is still half done Neharla, we must discover what Shivala wants to convey and do that, and that too, as early as possible" Parjanya said with much solicitude on his face.

The whole village people were on pedestal of hopes and excitement after this outcome. But apparently no one was able to perceive any clue from Shivala.

And that way one more hour passed.

Shivala also sat and took rest. Many of the people gathered here, it was the first ever sight of Shivala moving like this, as they had always seen him either laying on his wooden bed or sitting on that without making any movements.

One by one, Neharla, Parjanya, Kadrula and even Paataali tried to talk to Shivala. They again brought grass there and made Shivala touch it. For couple of moments Shivala got engaged with that but then again he was rubbing the floor and looking for something else.

Everyone now was losing patience, but no one had lost hope. What they all were now sure about was, the one fact that, Shivala has finally understood and realized that the witch grass threat has again struck on *Parubhumi.*

The Sun was setting quickly behind the mountains. People got tired waiting and so they also sat and started talking with one another about the possible ways. Only six eyes were watching Shivala's each movement and each break and those were Parjanya, Kadrula and Neharla.

Parjanya got up and lightened few earthen lamps, as it was now getting darker outside. He placed couple of earthen lamps in front of Shivala's room and couple of others in different directions to light up the area, as he used to do daily.

Other people also brought lamps from their home and few wooden torches from the Holy Stones field were brought there to light up as much area as possible.

So the area was all lightened up then. It was late evening but not a single person was ready to leave and go home. Children started sleeping in their parents' lap only.

Only Hanula, like every day, started chanting the evening prayer. And that very thing made the hope of people around here even stronger.

And Shivala got up and again started moving slowly in sitting position only. Parjanya again went close to him, just to protect his great great grandfather from any big hit with wall or pillar as well as from the burning fire close around.

Shivala spread his hands and again started searching for something the same way as he had been doing up till now.

Parjanya was moving just around him. Shivala went up to the door and touched it, and then he started searching for something again at the doorstep, so Parjanya carefully took away one of the earthen lamp from there to avoid any burns to Shivala.

Shivala slowly again moved to other direction, continuously trying to speak. Parjanya put back that lamp on its previous place again and got closer to Shivala watching his face, eyes, hands and each move.

One clue, one sign, that was all being sought from the heart of every person present there. Shivala again turn back and started taking help of the room outer walls. He reached the door frame and put his hand down on the doorstep corner a little quickly, and Parjanya was still on his back as Shivala turned around quickly, so before Parjanya could again move off the earthen lamp from there, Shivala had touched it.

And, at that very moment, the whole body of Shivala awakened like never before in decades! He quickly started vibrating his lips in order to speak, but as always he could not. But he held up the earthen lamp and raised it little high.

Fire.. Fire.. Fire.. voices came from all around there.

But Shivala now seemed as if he was able to see and understand everything, tried to rise up quickly, so at once, Parjanya helped him stand on his feet.

And again Shivala started taking his steps slowly, but somehow steadily and confidently now! He held his room's outer walls again and started walking slowly towards the back side of the room and immediately everyone was moving on to that direction with high breath.

And right in the backside of his room, suddenly Shivala stopped as if he had done it, he was breathing heavily just by walking this much distance. And in the lights of fire torches and earthen lamps, all could see Shivala holding the earthen lamp in one hand and showing the Mount *Busa* with his other hand pointed at *Busa*, so much steadily consciously and confidently, just like Mount *Busa* itself!

CHAPTER SEVENTEEN

Shivala was taken back to his room on his own daily wooden bed then, as he got almost fainted after hinting towards the Mount *Busa.*

Parjanya had not fed him since the previous night in order to make him feel hungry and to make him move on his own, so he can come across the grass around him.

But Shivala was so much feeble due to his age and on that day he took so much strain from noon to late evening; hence he got fainted at last.

"So it is almost clear and sure that there is some fire out there on Mount *Busa* and it can fight against the witch grass" Neharla said looking to all around.

"Still if any of you have different interpretation about what Shivala had shown, then please come forward and explain with reason and logic" he further added.

Once again the village men had gathered at the Holy Stones field, they all praised Parjanya a lot indeed.

Everyone now had true hope of surviving and saving Parubhumi from the demon now.
Almost everyone was of the same opinion that Shivala had hinted

for the "Holy Fire" that was in the *Busa* somewhere and needed to be brought from there. Because everyone knew that the normal domestic fire and flames had no effect and they just failed to burn out the witch grass since beginning.

This gathering took place on the same night just after putting Shivala back on his bed with so much gratitude from the *Parubhumi* people. Everyone was now hopeful and cheerful. It was after a long time that the people of *Parubhumi* had hopes in their eyes.

It was a late cold night but everyone was so excited that no one was feeling a slight cold actually.

"We need to go to *Busa* in search of that "Holy Fire" as quickly as possible," Parjanya said.

Suddenly it seemed as if Parjanya had taken charge of things ahead.

"Right, we should not waste time now, the witch grass has entered the village area already," Kadrula said with concern.

"Yes, every passing moment is critical now. I would request Hanula to arrange for *Parama* early morning tomorrow" Neharla said looking at Hanula, the village priest, who had joined all after finishing his daily prayer session.

"But this time we should not send all the *Walahas*, as there is a danger threat on the door now and we need men back here for any sudden and unknown challenge posed by the witch grass" Virajla said.

The silent fellow Virajla put up a very valid point this time.

"Yes very true, only three people shall go" Hanula said very authoritatively with his eyes closed that no one could question the number.

It was agreed to by Neharla promptly.

"Then we must send Kadrula, Parjanya and..."

"I will go, I will go please, Neharla let me please go" said Kala stopping Neharla saying further, with a deep pleading voice.

"But Kala, it is about sending *Walaha*s, and also, we need some experienced persons as well" Neharla said.

"No one has experience of going to *Busa* Mountain, has anyone?" asked Kala looking all around. And again said "Please Neharla let me go this time, I beg, I can't stay here. And if you deny, I swear I will throw myself in the witch grass" Kala said with immense agony.

Kadrula was watching Kala minutely all this while, and then he looked to Neharla and just nodded his head without saying anything.

Neharla therefore said "Okay then, Kala is going with Kadrula and Parjanya".

"Let's meet here tomorrow early in the morning for the *Parama*" said Neharla.
And everyone dispersed. After long time and for the first time post rising of witch grass in fact, people of *Parubhumi* were going back home from the Holy Stones field with a bit solid hope of fighting and defeating the witch grass.

But many of the *Walaha*s were surprised with the decision of Neharla for sending a non *Walaha* outside village and that too for such important task. Especially Velula and Buma were very upset when they were walking back to their home.

While walking back to home Parjanya was overwhelmed with the incidents that had taken place and those that would be taking place in coming days.

Would there be such Holy Fire, as Shivala has given hint of? It must have been long ago since Shivala himself is more than a century old man. What if there would be no such fire?

He, Kadrula and Kala would be out of village but what about the village people? And how would they find such Holy Fire in the vast *Busa*?

While thinking all such things Parjanya reached his home.

All the earthen lamps were out of oil and off. It was just darkness all around.

Parjanya first went to his room and got one earthen lamp and then he entered Shivala's room. He lightened the earthen lamp and put it beside Shivala's bed.

Shivala was fast asleep as always. Shivala, the son of *Parubhumi*, had done his part for his motherland already. Now it is his turn to do something for *Parubhumi*, Parjanya thought.

Shivala, please bless me, please give me your blessings. We need to find the Holy Fire you mentioned and guided about. Parjanya got overflowed in sentiments.

That night he could not catch the sleep till late. He had very thin memories about his parents. He was a kid when he lost both of them. He was brought up mainly by his grandparents. Somehow he was missing his parents deeply that night.

CHAPTER EIGHTEEN

"Yeah, I know it is different and important, very important this time. Let's hope that we find that Holy Fire that Shivala had guided about" Parjanya assertively told Vasudha.

It was dawn only and Vasudha had come to see off Parjanya.

"But there is no way left uncovered by the witch grass, so how will you people go out of the village now?" Vasudha was concerned about that.

"Yes you are right Vasudha but there is still a small patch of open land left at the Umi and other valleys somehow. We had visited that place yesterday only and checked properly, somehow the witch grass had not been able to cover the *Umi* valley area entirely. So we will leave by that place and then would go to the *Busa* mountain" Parjanya held Vasudha's face in his hands, of which, he could see only her two eyes properly.

It was decided that Parjanya, Kadrula and Kala would leave with the rising Sun. As it was not known how much time or how many days it would take to find the Holy Fire, so everything had to be done in hurry.

"Vasudha I guess you should return now, I too will leave. We will meet again soon. Please take care of yourself, Shivala and all around you. I don't know what future is looming for us or for you all here but yes we have to fight and find a way in order to survive and win. Always remember that I am there with you wherever you are" Parjanya hugged Vasudha tightly.

The Holy water pot held by Hanula was shining with the early morning Sun rays.
It was a different atmosphere and emotion today compared to the normal time when *Walaha*s used to leave after *Usa*, every villager was present there wishful as well as unrest in their hearts. Hanula handed over the water pot first to Kadraula and then Kadrula passed it to Parjanya and then Parjanya passed it to Kala. Kala missed it a little and some water got dropped.

And thus, three of them went down the valley after holding the holy water pot in hand at a time. Once they got down the valley, Kala handed over the Holy water pot to Kadrula and it was placed on the earth and it was to be taken back when they returned from their journey and entered the village again.

All three men were ready to leave towards *Busa* Mountain now.

It was conveyed by Hanula this time that Mother Nature had permitted them to leave the village as it wasn't a *Walaha* trip. Hence no such ritual was always done for *Walaha* trip.

All the three men were just sprinkled with holy water on them. And as soon as one bird twitted, they started down from the *Umi* valley.

Very carefully they crossed the small patches at *Umi* valley and started a downward journey.
Neharla, Hanula and other remaining *Walaha*s kept an eye on them till they receded behind the dense vegetation in deep valley.

Neharla and everyone came back to Holy Stones Field after sending off the Trio for the greatest search, the search of survival. As usual there was a silence. In fact atmosphere all around was lifeless in its kind. The only constant sound that was breaking the silence, since days now, was the cacophony of the witch grass.

Neharla somehow felt incomplete without Kadrula this time. Prior it was different when Kadrula would go out of village for days during the *Walaha* trips. But this time it was a different condition. Kadrula was a rock solid support to Neharla in any testing and trying situation apart from the daily village business.

"What are you thinking Neharla" asked Hanula, seeing Neharla lost in deep thoughts.

"Nothing is left to think about Hanu, it all depends on Mother Nature's will and wish now. If the trio could find the Holy Fire and can manage to bring it safely here, we will survive or else as the Mother Nature wishes" said Neharla with pretty dignified smile on his face.

"Jhanula, cows are not eating grass" Adhu and Buka came straight to Jhanula who also was sitting along with Neharla and Hanula at the Holy stone field.

"Oh I think I haven't sprinkled the *Reli* on the grass today morning, I forgot to actually. Let's go, we should make them eat well" Jhanula went with Adhu and Buka towards the *Gaushala*.

Virajla came there with some hot milk for Neharla and Hanula. He handed over them carefully and then served some herbal liquid to the other men there. All started sipping. This herbal liquid was the specialty of Virajla, everyone knew that. In fact Virajla was next to Jhanula in terms of knowledge of herbs and vegetation.

"How much time would it be for them to come back from *Busa*" Saral couldn't resist asking this question, which was, in fact, on everyone's mind there.

It was deep silence there and with that silence, it too was a question that who would answer it!

After few moments, Hanula said "We all here and they three there are pacing with time Saral, so no one can say yes, but what we can do is we can do our best for our people whatsoever it is". Everyone started sipping from their pots again.

And there in the village, Paataali had initiated the evacuation of *Bhandaras* and *Gaushala* set ups. She had foreseen that soon that had to be carried out anyhow, and with time the village people are likely to be even more lifeless and depressed, hence it was better to direct them towards work now when they still can give optimum output. All the women and men had started resituating the cattle and stuffs in the centre area of the village. New artificial waterways and streams were being planned to construct. Virajla was the man behind that notion.

It was as if people of *Parubhumi* were determined not to give up on the witch grass till their last breath. They knew that time was an important factor in this fight now. The longer time they stand their ground keeping themselves safe, the more chances of their survival were there. Just by the hope of getting the Holy Fire, the spirit of people of *Parubhumi* was high as sky now.

Parjanya and Kala were standing a side watching Kadrula. They had reached at the foothills of *Busa* Mountain. It was noon and they had been continuously walking to reach there.

Before putting a foot on *Busa*, Kadrula stood silently for a while closing his eyes and joining both of his hands and then he bowed to *Busa*. Both, Parjanya and Kala also did the same as Kadrula did.

Kadrula opened his eyes and put his foot on Mount *Busa*. Parjanya and Kala followed him. Just like the *Walahas* they also were walking in the linear manner one after another.

"We have to keep moving at night time and in daytime as well. In fact only that will help us more" Kadrula said.

"Because the Holy Fire that Shivala had hinted about, must be the one burning day and night and we would be able to see it easily in the night time in darkness" he further added.

"You are right Kadrula, we have to keep moving day and night" Parjanya said.

As always, as a leader, Kadrula was walking ahead, followed by Parjanya and Kala.

After walking for some time, they entered the green Jungle of *Busa*, the Jungle that they could always see as a small green patch only, on the *Busa* from far away. But now when they actually had been there, only then they could realise how dense, green and vast Jungle it was and almost seeming endless. There were different kind of trees, birds and flowers in there.

Kadrula, Parjanya and Kala all were walking while searching around constantly. However Kadrula only was searching continuously, whereas Parjanya and Kala were mesmerized and they were amazed with the landscape.

There was no trail there on *Busa*, so the trio had to walk heedful. As decided by Kadrula at the start of journey, they were walking in circular manner and in ascending order, in order to get the maximum view in order to find the Holy Fire.

Kadrula stopped at one water stream and after a small conversation as always, he drank water from it. It was afternoon then but the entire Jungle was so thick that the sunlight hardly could reach to the soil there. And therefore it was much darker there.

Parjanya and Kala also drank water just after Kadrula finished. And then Kadrula walked up to a huge tree and climbed a little on it. And after asking for permission from the tree, he cut off some leaves and fruits from that tree. He brought them down with him and gave it to Parjanya and Kala too. And all three of them had their first lunch on *Busa*.

After resting for some time, the trio again started off. While walking on *Busa* they realised that there was almost the plain surface there. Though it was the biggest mountain, but it wasn't steep climbing there, hence walking was much easier.

"Kadrula, I am feeling so much live and fresh out here, I mean particularly after living Parbhumi" Parjanya said.

"Same with me" Kala said at once before Kadrula could respond anything to it.

"Yes Parjanya, it's because of the witch grass' ill effect. We feel less alive once it is around. The witch grass sucks life from everything that is alive. I hope the people of *Parubhumi* fight and survive in that battle till we get back there with the Holy Fire" Kadrula said looking around.

"The Holy Fire must be with some human being, right? or is it here burning on its own?" Kala asked.

Kadrula stopped, looked back smilingly and said "we know nothing Kala, but most probably the Holy Fire must be here being preserved by someone".

"Then it can't be in the open, it has to be in some kind of safe place under shelter or in some den" Parjanya said walking carefully on the small stones which were ready to roll anytime.

"Exactly, that's what I wanted to say" Kala said.

The trio kept on walking and looking around while talking too.

"And also, if someone is preserving it, then that someone also must be needing certain things to sustain, like water, food etc. So we have to be extra cautious at water streams and edible fruit trees areas and other such promising places" Kadrula said smilingly.

"Yes yes Kadrula, you are absolutely right, now I think we would find the Holy Fire for sure" Kala said with enthusiasm.

It was much colder and inky now. It was just evening time but it looked as if Night had already fallen on *Busa* Mountain. But the trio still kept moving. Now they were not keeping much distance between them while walking though.

As directed by Kadrula, they had fixed their directions to watch carefully for each of them. Parjanya was to watch East and Kala was to watch West, whereas Kadrula had to concentrate on North and South both. *Busa* became even livelier in the dark night. The night wildlife was alive and active then and hence the trio was careful about not being the disturbance to them. There was jet darkness and six eyes together were searching for just one thing, some light, but that wasn't to be seen yet.

Kadrula looked up at the sky and watched stars for a while. Kadrula could perfectly predict the exact day and night time periods by just watching the position of shadows and stars. When he finally got to see some open sky, he finally decided to halt the move and take rest.

"This is the time when entire wildlife, even the predators and preys too, take rest, halt and become inactive, hence we must respect this stillness and nature as whole" he explained while laying down on the bare land patch.

Parjanya and Kala also got down and sat in a resting position in a while. They were feeling so much relieved just by sitting down, that they dozed off laying over a nearby big tree trunk.

Suddenly the trio woke up, as there was some commotion nearby. It was dawn almost then. All the three of them got up and again started off.

Just walking and walking while looking around. During the day time it was little different than the way they used to search at night. Now they would look for some place where someone could be dwelling. And also, mainly the places around any water stream, which were numerous there actually and any place that could speak up safety from animals and closer to the edible fruit trees, were the potential and probable places where they could find the Holy Fire as per Kadrula's view.

Parjanya and Kala had noticed after sometime that Kadrula was all the time watching east and west directions as well, which was actually not his job. The moment Kadrula would slow down a little in walking, both Parjanya and Kala would presume it to be the place with some potential and hence they too would closely search there.

It was the third day's Night and the trio was walking and walking. And now they reached to little height. And it was less dense there now. Since they were walking in the spiral pattern, they were taking circular routes of *Busa* in ascending manner. They were slow in covering the distance and mass but they were very much precise in scanning things and areas at the same time.

It was sheer darkness all around and the trio kept walking in search of any small light or flame. Only Kadrula was holding a small wooden torch to see through the way ahead of him, rest two just had to walk the same way keeping watch on different directions.

"See it is there" Parjanya shouted suddenly, pointing to far upwards to his left.

Kadrula stopped and looked back at Parjanya.

Kala too came to Parjanya in big long steps.

"It was there actually" Parjanya now said, as if he himself was not finding it there right now.
"Parjanya, it could be an illusion too, as we sleep less nowadays. And moreover, it happens especially when we desperately search for something and don't find it" Kadrula came to Parjanya and petted on his shoulders.

Parjanya felt ashamed a little. But Kadrula as if he too wanted a break suddenly said,
"I think we should take a small break here only, we may pin point that place as well, so that we can have more careful look there" saying this Kadrula looked up the stars and as if got something.

"No Kadrula, as we know, night is the best possible time to find the Holy Fire, so we must continue" Parjanya said with little regret.

"And also we don't have much time to waste as well. Three days are completed already, God knows what might have been the situation back at *Parubhumi*" Parjanya added with a big sigh.

"That's true too. Let's keep it up. We may take rest only at our daily fixed time" Kadrula started off at once.

And the trio continued their search again.

CHAPTER NINETEEN

Tchi.... Tchi.... Tchi... was the only constant sound in *Parubhumi* now. Every single living object was feeling like hell due to this piercing sound.

The witch grass had grown up to the sheep height almost on all the sides of *Parubhumi* now. And the taller witch grass had a stronger ill effect on the living objects. The witch grass had engulfed half of the village land by now.

Many homes, including Kadrula's and Velu's, were completely engulfed by the witch grass, as they were in the village border area.

The village *Bhandaras* were now under the witch grass. So shifting of all the food and grass for cattle and other common village goods and stuffs to the open land and houses of people, was proven to be a timely and good decision indeed.

The cows, buffaloes and all other domesticated animals were now in the mid of the village, tied up around the houses. So now there was less open space left in the village.

Somehow from the day when Kadrula, Parjanya and Kala had left in search of the Holy fire, the witch grass had started growing faster ever. It was now few steps away from Parjanya's, Tatu's and couple of more homes. Hence those homes were vacated in advance as well. The witch grass was now making progress day and night.

The presence of witch grass was life sucking, all the villagers by now knew this. People of *Parubhumi* were all sick and slug all the time. They turned barren with no inclination or wish or intention of doing anything whatsoever.

They hardly would talk to each other. All the time they were indolent and down mentally. And this was not only with humans but also with cattle and other animals. All the living objects under the influence of witch grass were feeling soulless. Even the trees which prior used to give fruits and flowers had stopped giving. Moreover, they were shading their leaves and getting dried out and dying slowly. The *Parubhumi* was turning into graveyard.

But there were few who were having the mental strength and edge to overcome the lifelessness spread in the entire village atmosphere.

Virajla and Paataali were such iron-willed people. Others were Mohan Hanula, his wife Sitili and Jhanula.

Paataali along with Hanula's wife Sitili had started meditation sessions and activity class sessions for women of the village. Each day the women of *Parubhumi* would meditate in the morning and evening. As per Paataali it was necessary to keep the women of village mentally strong as they were the prime influencers of their family. Moreover, they would do the cooking at the common kitchen created recently in separate area in the village. This was the idea of Sitili to keep women of the village together, so as to keep their spirit alive and high with company of others like them. Since the field and farms work wasn't to be taken up any longer and the women of *Parubhumi* were habituated working hard and at par with their men counterparts, they had to be kept engaged.

Paataali had gotten that if any individual, especially a woman, is left alone for little longer time, she would fall into depression and would be the victim of mental disorders due to the heaviness of witch grass' negative vibrations in the atmosphere all over.

Same was with Virajla. He had taken charge of men. Virajla may speak less but act great. He could foresee that the witch grass would one day encircle the entire village, so not only food grain for human and fodder for cattle would be important and critical, but the other most important commodity would be drinking water.

So from the day the three men left for the Holy Fire, Virajla had formed teams of village men to look for the possible and sudden threats from witch grass. And thus, he could keep the young and older men of the village woven in work, and in that way saved them from becoming depressed.

Both Paataali and Virajla, the husband wife duo, had been able to keep the negative effects of the witch grass at bay successfully this way. They knew that the only way to do that was to keep people engaged in some useful work and keeping them connected among one another.

Vasudha and her friends were all sitting together silently looking at the *Busa* Mountain. *Busa* was the hope for People of *Parubhumi* for their survival now. Vasudha most of the time of a day would sit seeing *Busa*. Though she knew, but she at the same time couldn't resist the notion that she might be able to see Parjanya suddenly anytime there.

Suddenly Vasudha said "Will they ever be back? It has been six days since they have left and still they are not back, something might have happened to them".

"Yeah they have to face a lot of things there, who knows. And if they are not going to come back, we are all going to die here"

Mahi said.

"Who says they won't come back? who says we are going to die?" Paataali was right there like a fresh air wave.

"This witch grass would never be able to harm us a little even, forget about dying. We all are going to survive and that's for sure. Don't you all remember? We have already defeated it once in past" Paataali said in one go with her usual metallic voice.

Sitili who came there with Paataali, was holding one container which was creating a smoke. There was fire burning inside the container and of course Sitili had put some flowers and petals of Himalayan plant inside the container in the burning fire, hence the smoke was having a special fragrance.

Sitili just kept on moving and walking everywhere around in order to spread the smoke and fragrance in the maximum area.

And yeah that smoke had a very strong and positive effect on anyone smelling it and inhaling it. That was *Siruha*! One of the most pious and strong positive Himalayan plant. Its vapor would infuse life and liveliness along with positivity in the atmosphere and into every living object present there in that atmosphere.

Sitili had to walk and move through very narrow space as the village people and other livestock, goods and stuffs were all confined to a very limited area now.

But for the time being everything was alive. The cattle started making their usual noises. People started feeling like doing some good work and they all started having thoughts even. *Siruha* was showing the positive effects on every live thing.

Vasudha and all the other girls at once started feeling so nice. They again started off for their routine job and activities of feeding the cattle and other live stocks.

Sitili also walked through the area where cattle and other livestock were situated. All those animals were tied around houses and nearby open spaces. There was a mess like scenario there. As there wasn't much open space around. It was all congested.

The witch grass was growing horizontally and vertically at even pace, and thus engulfing everything coming its way. Thus the circle of open space around village was reducing day and night inch by inch. Hence everything had to be brought in the mid and away from the witch grass vicinity, in order to save the same.

But everybody knew that the effect of Siruha was momentous only until it is again burnt in the fire. And they knew that *Siruha* was in scarcity and hence had to be used with circumscribe. And therefore Sitili had taken up that onus in her own hands. She very well knew when to start using *Siruha*.

It was like the People of *Parubhumi* were trained animals now. As soon as they started feeling well they started working for themselves, cattle and other livestock as well.

They would even cook and eat during that good feeling time period. As, once that *Siruha* effect is gone, they all would sink into lifelessness trance again.

So, for now, the *Parubhumi* was live again. Men and women were on the work and on the move. Children too would play a little in a limited area, mostly with the animals.

There was the tchi.. tchi.. tchi.. Noise too, but for now nobody would care about it.

Just *Siruha* was there omnipresent, for now.

CHAPTER TWENTY

Rain had stopped. And they knew that they have to restart as soon as possible. Rain had forced them to halt for couple of hours. In the beginning they tried to continue anyhow but after climbing some distance, they realised that the land had become very slippery and they can't tread with confidence on such surface. So the trio decided to take a break from the endless walking. They took shelter under one big hanging boulder and that had provided them good protection from rain too.

And they started again after some time. Watchfully, step by step.

"Today is the seventh day Kadrula" said Parjanya.

And there was a deep grief in that voice. Kala almost was about to burst into tears, as he was walking last watching his assigned direction, none of the two walking ahead of him was able to notice that.

Kadrula just looked back to Parjanya and gave a smile and continued walking.

All the three very well knew that if they fail to find the Holy Fire in time, it would be worthless then. They had to find the Holy Fire and that too within time limit predicted by Hanula and Neharla, to save their land from the twitch grass.

The trio was on tenterhook snow. And it had become strenuous to move fast now as the land turned slippery. Moreover, hundreds of seasonal water streams had come alive on *Busa* Mountain after the rain. Hence other sounds were almost inaudible.
New species of animals were also encountered which up to then were deep in the Forest. The Trio now had to take every precaution of safety for them since the canvas had changed after rain. Everything was wet and dripping.

They kept walking and walking and walking till evening. Today none of them thought of food even. They would just drink water from some nearby stream and keep moving.

Today too, they came across another pond on the way. They, as decided, spent considerable time there for searching the surrounding area for any possible human habitat, but even today too they were greatly disappointed and had to leave from there with no signs of Holy Fire and its possessor.

The Sun was preparing to set. Parjanya looked at it and felt thankful somehow, as he believed that it was effortless to search for Holy Fire in the dark than in the daylight.

And suddenly, Kadrula stopped walking. He was looking little upwards to his left. And he wasn't looking actually, he was trying to listen carefully in fact. Parjanya and Kala came tiptoed to Kadrula.

Kadrula signaled them to keep quiet. During all these days, Kadrula was not seen this electrified and suspicious about anything.

Couple of more minutes elapsed. They stood immobile. And again Kadrula made the same excited face and this time it reflected in his eyes as well. As if he was clearly listening to some chatter or voices. Parjanya and Kala were also trying hard to listen to any thin sound other than birds' chirping, streams flowing and sometimes breaking of some twigs but both of them were unable to hear anything unusual.

And then after sometime, Kadrula started moving to that direction from where he heard some sounds. There was not much plain land in that direction and it was an elevated part too. Kadrula left the plain land and straight away started scaling to upward direction. There was a heap of excitement and enthusiasm on Kadrula's face, when he was leaping stone by stone and boulder by boulder.

Seeing him, both Parjanya and Kala started following Kadrula feet by feet.

However it was proven to be appreciably a steep climbing but all the three were so enlivened that they quickly negotiated all that. Kadrula was so much quick in negotiating whatever came in his way while climbing that, Parjanya and Kala were just forced to be at his pace in fact.

And after climbing like that for half an hour, first Kadrula and then Parjanya and Kala one by one reached to a flatland.

That was again a lush Jungle there. But somehow all of them had a very strong feeling as if someone else was also there around only and they were not alone there.
The Sun was hasty in setting fast in the west now. So darkness was falling quickly. The wooden torches, the Trio was using every night, were all got little wet and damp. So when Parjanya took his one out, Kadrula, with a small gesture, denied him. Parjanya at once put it back.

Kadrula carefully kept looking on around as if he was scanning the surrounding surface feet by feet. For nearly half an hour he did so and then he came and sat with Parjanya and Kala.

"Could any of you hear that sound?" Finally Kadrula asked with a whisper. He kept his voice so much low as if he just was talking to himself only. "No I couldn't" Parjanya and Kala both said almost simultaneously with the same frequency of voice as Kadrula's.

"That was certainly the sound made by some human. It cannot be mistaken with any animal or bird or any other thing for sure" Kadrula said with sheer confidence.
And listening to this Parjanya and Kala both got back their breath of joy because they knew that Kadrula is a senior and hence the most experienced one here as well as second most senior after Neharla in *Parubhumi*, with numerous skills and an encyclopedia of knowledge about Nature and life as a whole, hence he could never be erroneous.

"So what are we going to do now? Will we look around for that in the night?" asked Kala.
"In my opinion, No. Tonight we should do nothing except sticking at one place and keeping our eyes and ears wide open. I am sure we are close to the Holy Fire. We will take enough rest tonight, harness our senses, as we haven't slept properly for last 6-7 nights and whole last night in particular" Kadrula replied.

"Can't we call loudly for help? Whoever is there would come to us" Kala asked eagerly.
"No, I don't think we should do that. Prior, I too thought of that Kala but somehow I feel that whosoever having the Holy Fire, might not have good terms with *Parubhumi*. I don't know why but my intuition is like this. And the Saints who possess the power or such pious and unique treasure, never prefer to be disturbed and meet people, most of the times" Kadrula replied with his murmuring voice.

Kadrula looked at Parjanya who was silent at all these and asked him "You want to say something Parjanya?"

Parjanya, as if hesitant to say, said "Should we not try to find the Holy Fire in the dark and night? Would it not be easy for us to find it during night?" And after saying Parjanya found himself being offensive, as he used to revere Kadrula right from his adolescent age.

But Kadrula, as usual, with immense love and affection for Parjanya, said "You are very true according to your logic Parjanya but what I am feeling from within is, we no longer need to be logical. Time has come to be faithful now to find out something which is here, around only and is ready to bless us". Both Parjanya and Kala had never heard such voice of Kadrula before. Parjanya bowed to Kadrula and so did Kala afterwards.

The sun had arisen in the East. The Jungle had woken up again. And the Trio, who had their best sleep after so many days, was on toes.

The Trio decided to go for the search in separate directions to cover the maximum area at one time. And it was decided that if any of them get some sign or clue, he will make the Himalayan Peafowl sound three times, as there were ample Peafowl around.

Kadrula, Parjanya and Kala went off to the different directions after wishing each other the best luck. As all of them knew that this was the most critical phase of their journey now, they all were little emotional about that. It was the matter of saving their motherland. They were walking and checking around assiduously. Any unusual or special sign or sight was all they were looking for. Any sign. What they were looking for all these days was almost at arm's length and yet hidden. Hence they were so much thrilled and cautious at the same time.

Kadrula had taken the very direction from which he had heard that sound of some human activity. He was trickling and watchful all around. He knew that whoever was there must have been just around at this moment and might be watching him wandering as well. This was a little more dense forest, with medium to small boulders all around covered with green vegetation.

Kadrula was scanning every inch now with his experienced eyes. Anywhere, two or more boulders or some dense vegetation could be the potential place. He was looking at every piece of stone and each tree or plant and grass patch carefully. He would pause and recheck if he finds any tiny sign by any mean.

So was with Parjanya and Kala. They too were searching everything closely as instructed by Kadrula. Kala was more eager to find the Holy Fire before the rest of the two could. So he was checking quickly as well. He was trying to move and look through the small plants and boulders as well. Somehow he was much effusive during all through this journey.

But Parjanya was by now getting much clear and sure about where that 'someone' could well be. Somehow his inner was forcing him to believe that the Holy Fire was somewhere beneath the ground. He was putting his feet with much care and precision. He wasn't looking around less and watching down carefully all the time. Every small stone, any little bushes, roots of mammoth trees, everything.

It has to be almost here. Just around here. These very words were ringing in the ears of all three of them right at that moment. Kadrula had checked the small water trickle for the third time now, as that was the very place from where he heard that sound of some human activity. He had no doubts of someone being around there recently.

And suddenly Peoh.. Peoh.. Peoh.. sound came. It was from Parjanya's direction.

And Kadrula ran to Parjanyain a blink.

CHAPTER TWENTY-ONE

It had been more than two hours now. In couple of more hours it would be an afternoon then. The Trio was sitting and waiting quietly without any movements for the last 2 hours now. Kala was at his highest level of uneasiness and unrest from among three of them. He would look at Kadrula almost every minute. Parjanya also was not at all at ease, as he too knew that very precious and important time was passing by. But he managed to keep calm as he always was having great amount of faith in Kadrula.

Kadrula was sitting quietly, looking straight without blinking his eyes.

And what he was looking at? He was just looking at that! Yes it was there! The Holy Fire!
This was the place they wanted to be at since last one week. Yes, Parjanya was the one who found out this place where the Holy Fire was burning.

And it was there right in front of them. The Holy Fire! It was looking like the sole source of light in the whole Universe. It was quite quite different from the common fire they all had seen till date. It was rather some aura.

As Parjanya had a kind of clairvoyance that the Holy Fire should be somewhere beneath the ground they are walking, he started focusing downwards more than around. And by chance his one foot got a little touch of the *Risa* plant string that was dry, as it generally seems. And Parjanya got stuck there at once.

Right from the childhood Parjanya knew that the *Risa* plant is so much strong that it can hold up even his own size boulder in the air with only one string of it. *Parubhumi* people too used the *Risa* to tie things and bind stuffs strongly. And he was well aware of tying the animals and cattle when needed to tie them strongly for some medical emergency.

Parjanya picked up the Risa string and pulled it gently, it was a long string leading Parjanya ahead and ahead in one direction, and finally its one end was found tied with some wooden block made of a huge tree bark and covered with leaves. And it was obvious that it was the entrance of some place underneath.

Parjanya immediately made sound of Peafowl for three times to call Kadrula and Kala. And three of them then entered the cave one by one.

And that was in fact a cave in the cave. There were several caves in fact. The trio looked into one by one and found it in the last cave. It was there, situated in some strange container which looked like a globe.

And he was there as well. The one who possessed the Holy Fire. A man who was appearing ageless, sitting right there with his eyes closed and legs crossed just like the mountain, still and calm.

Kadrula put his one finger on his lips and asked the rest of the two to keep silence.
They went closer to that man who had huge beard and was sitting on the ground in front of them. The men still didn't open his eyes; neither had he made any movements.

The man was wearing the clothes made from a tree bark. It was difficult to say if he was breathing even.

Kadrula with a small sign asked Parjanya and Kala to sit and wait patiently and he himself too sat in front of that saint.

And the Trio started waiting then, sitting quietly without any movement.

Few more hours passed. They weren't able to make out but the Sun must have set completely by now, they thought. Kadrula too was a bit uneasy now. All were sitting looking at the bearded man and sometimes the Holy Fire.

And as suden that bearded man opened his eyes. He first looked at Kadrula and then Parjanya and Kala. Without speaking a single word he got up from his place and went to another cave to his left.

He came out with some kind of wooden vessel and then went out of the cave, as if he was not bothering about the presence of three unknown people around him.

The Trio only kept watching what the bearded man was doing.

Once he had gone out, Kala at once said "Kadrula our significant time has been wasted. We have to hurry now. Please tell him everything as soon as he comes back"
And just at that time Kadrula once again heard the sound that he heard yesterday around this time only.

Kadrula looked at Parjanya, Parjanya at once said "Yeah I have heard it this time".
"We can't force or compel him for anything, all we can do is, we can request him. So we have to have some forbearance now, else all our efforts and endeavors can well go in vain" said Kadrula looking at Kala authoritatively.

The bearded man was back after couple of minutes. There were some fruits and leaves in his vessel when he came back.

The bearded man added some water into that vessel and stir it with one small bunch of some roots, and then ate that and drank the water after that.

He then sat on his place again with crossed legs and looked at Kadrula.

Kadrula joined both his hands together and said "Hey great Soul, the possessor of the Holy Fire, I am Kadrula, son of the pious *Parubhumi*".

The bearded man raised an eyebrow while hearing the name *Parubhumi*.

"We are all in a dire situation in *Parubhumi*. A kind of evil grass has erupted around the village. The grass engulfs and kills everything that it catches. Nothing could destroy that witch grass. One of the eldest man in our *Parubhumi* could somehow hint us about this Holy Fire, as this Holy Fire only can destroy that witch grass, we suppose. Hence we three left the village seven days ago in search of this Holy Fire. The witch grass must have grown even further into the village by now and could have harmed people and other living objects. All our hopes and lives of people of *Parubhumi* and other living objects there hinged on your blessings now, we need your blessings and help" Kadrula finished with his head bowing down.
"Oh Shiva.. Shiva must have told you about this Holy Fire. Shiva is still there? Is he still there? How is he? I have all the sympathy for your people, but I can't come there now. Once I was asked to leave from there. I was humiliated and ousted. So I left from there with this Holy Fire. Shiva humiliated me. Perhaps Mother Nature must have destined this very situation for *Parubhumi*" said the bearded man with graceful smile on his face.

Parjanya at once got up from his place, bowed and put his head on the feet of the bearded man and pleaded "Hey great Saint and possessor of Holy Fire, the descendant of Shivala, his great great grandson is begging for pardon on his behalf. Hey descendant of the greats who set up and prosper the *Parubhumi* with their blessings, please grant an amnesty to us, please forgive Shivala. Please show your kindness and save us all. People of *Parubhumi*, people of the land setup by your ancestors, need your help and blessings".

The bearded man closed his eyes for a while. He opened his eyes, smiled, put a hand on Parjanya's head which was still at his feet and then said "Okay come, get up, I am coming with you to *Parubhumi*".

There were uncontrollable tears in the eyes of Kadrula, Parjanya and Kala simultaneously.

Now Kadrula got up and said bowing to the bearded man, "We need to leave instantly; every passing moment is dangerous for our people".

"Yes, we are leaving just now" said the bearded man putting his hand on Kadrula's shoulders.

The bearded man again sat in front of the holy fire facing it and started chanting the Holy shlokas for sometimes.

Suddenly the Holy Fire started burning brighter. And then the bearded man picked up the Holy Fire in his bare hands without any vessel or container as if he were to hold the bunch of flowers.

"He also took his arm bag, made of big dry leaves, one wooden stick, and started walking to the outer of the cave. He was a lightning-quick in everything he would do.

The Trio at once followed him.

There was dark outside. But the Holy Fire was generating some different and divine light than the wooden torches the Trio was using up to now.

"It might have taken 7 days for you to reach here but I can take you merely in a day to your place from where you have come here" said the bearded man smilingly.

"Just keep following me anyhow, without any doubt or fear" he added.

The bearded man was walking really at a lightning speed.

"Someone from your village must have broken the rules of *Parubhumi*, else the witch grass couldn't have such chance" said the bearded man looking back while walking.

The bearded man was leading the Trio surprisingly straight and downwards from different direction. He was walking so fast that the Trio had to almost run to match his steps.

The route bearded man had taken was easier to walk, as if it was a walkway.
They continued walking in the same one direction and pace till dawn. And during this journey they encountered many animals and reptiles in the jungle. But none of them was seeming a threat to them this time. All the other creatures were quite friendly that all of them gave way through their habitats even. Kadrula somehow felt that the route taken by the bearded man was the most dangerous one in terms of facing and meeting the Jungle animals, including ferocious reptiles. But there wasn't any sign of animosity in any creature.

At dawn, the bearded man took a small pause at a particular place. He turned towards East with the Holy Fire in his hands and then bowed down in that direction with both his hands lifted towards the sky.

The trio too followed the same gesture. During the break none of them spoke a single word but the Trio had the same unique feeling, and that was, none of them was tired a bit. They all were feeling as fresh as they had started the journey in the very beginning.

They started again. And now the slopes were less on their way down. It was more like walking on the plain surface. But still Kadrula was not able to have an idea about the route they had come so far. Kadrula had kept a note of each important detail about the route they had come from and this route was not at all matching with the original one they had taken while reaching here.

It was noon now. The bearded man again stopped walking. He looked at all three and then smiled and asked "Are you all famished?"

Straight away three of them denied. Yet the bearded man asked Parjanya to get four leaves of the tree they were standing and resting under. They had again taken a break for lunch.

Parjanya was little surprised about the number of leaves asked for.

"Yeah, one leaf for each one of us" said the bearded man.

"And of course you must be knowing, since you are from Parubhumi, always ask for the permission from the Tree, before you take anything from them" the bearded man added, smiling ear to ear.

Parjanya went bowing to the bearded man; he came back and gave four leaves to bearded man.

The bearded man asked Parjanya to hold them for a while in his hands. And during that he closed his eyes and chanted few

Holy Mantras.

He opened his eyes and asked Parjanya to give one leaf to each one of them for eating.

Parjanya gave each one by his own hands and lastly he himself ate one leaf.

Parjanya felt that the taste of that leaf was heavenly. It could never be described in words but yes it was heavenly indeed. It had all the tastes that were known yet it was beyond words really.

And though they were damn hungry, just only one leaf had pacified their hunger to the core.

The bearded man looked at the Trio and just smiled and again started walking ahead of them.

"We are just close to the *Parubhumi* now" said the bearded man.

All the other three men were greatly surprised hearing that.

Kadrula, Parjanya and Kala all three had some unknown feeling listening to this and they just were short of words to describe that actually.

"No it's not like what you say", the bearded man told Kadrula with his patented smile.

"It has to be placed and established on its original place first and only then it can be used" the bearded man added.

They had reached to the border of *Parubhumi* with the Holy Fire. It was late evening by then. And upon reaching there, they saw from far that the witch grass had grown up to the height that could engulf two men, one on one, in height. They couldn't see anything from there.

And when Kadrula requested the bearded man to burn out the witch grass with the Holy Fire then the bearded man clarified.

And that revelation was highly disappointing for the Trio. Because as per the need, they required to enter the village by crossing the witch grass which was sheer impossible now.

Tchi.... Tchi... Tchi.... The same old, infamous and horrific sound again. The Trio was despondent now. Somehow a very sad and disappointing feeling wrapped them and thus the trio were all sunk in it..

All of them were just looking at the direction of village without blinking an eye in a deep grief. The bearded man had sat on one small boulder with closed eyes and crossed legs facing the witch grass and *Parubhumi*. None of the trio could realise when they fell asleep.

It was Kadrula who was up immediately with the first Ray of the Sun. The bearded man was doing meditation facing the different direction, little away from them holding the Holy Fire in his hands.

Parjanya and Kala too woke up in a while. The witch grass was now clearly visible. It had diminished its sound since it was sun light all around.

"We need to find some way to enter the village Kadrula, this witch grass has grown ten times higher than what we had seen it last" Parjanya said with great disappointment.

"Yes, with this height, we can't cross it simply without getting caught" said Kadrula.
"We need to take a round in this surrounding, if there is a lesser height patch anywhere, we can try to enter from there" said Kala, his voice was all changed.

Kala said this with a very different tone; both Kadrula and Parjanya were little surprised listening to it.

They had in fact come down from little different direction from *Busa*. But now in the day light they found that they were at the doorstep of *Parubhumi*precisely.

After a while, the bearded man came there. They all discussed the situation and decided to find the lower height patch of witch grass to cross it.

And as ago, the bearded man just asked them to follow him and started walking.
Once again the journey started. It was so resentful to be at the doorstep of their Motherland and not being able to enter it. Desperately they were walking close to witch grass, looking for any lower height patch. But unfortunately the witch grass had grown drastically higher all around by then.

At mid day, they reached to the valley. And Parjanya of course recognised it. That was the valley of roots. How could he forget this valley! Thoughtit seemed to be the other side of it.

"We need to go through the valley" the bearded man said.

And they started walking down the valley but so was the Sun seemed to be doing and that too with little more hurry!

None of the trio had ever been here before, despite living so close to this place. As their *Walaha* route was different and fixed. Since ages they would go out and enter the village with fixed routs.

The bearded man, as usual, was walking much quicker than the Trio. It was the late afternoon now, the trio was getting disheartened badly now, as they were at the doorstep of their Motherland but were unable to enter it and save their own people.

And suddenly they saw the bearded men stopped at one spot at the elevation of the valley. Kadrula first reached to the bearded man, followed by Parjanya and Kala.
The bearded man had found the very rare patch actually, where the witch grass was not grown that higher yet. This was really something very encouraging and optimistic, as all the other areas they had seen were all covered with very tall witch grass, almost the size of two person, one on one.

"From here we can try to enter" said Parjanya with very hopeful tone.

"Yeah the witch grass is really shorter here, we can enter from this spot" Kala at once said.

"But how come only this patch has shorter witch grass? As there is a taller witch grass all round" Kadrula asked.

"*Siruha*, yes, that's what I was checking all around, *Siruha* would have given up after a lot of resistance to the witch grass, this must have been a *Siruha* patch once" said the bearded man with his as always smile.

"Yeah of course the witch grass is shorter here but it is almost more than one man's length wide. How can we jump this distance as it is almost on the verge of the valley. We need to run a little to jump off this distance in one go" the bearded man explained with no expressions on his face.

And there was very disappointing silence there. All the three men there were broken down badly again.

Every moment that was passing was painful for them, they could well imagine the situation with people inside their beloved village.

"Kadrula, please show us some way out please, we can't keep waiting like this" Parjanya pleaded on the verge of crying.

But before Kadrula could speak or say something, Kala, with heavy steps, went to the verge of small witch grass patch. The way Kala had walked past the three men; they all just saw him with little surprise. Kala suddenly turned around facing his companions and then loudly and with so much divergent voice said "You, the most respected and the bearer of Holy Fire, Kadrula, my childhood ideal and Parjanya, my younger brother", Kala was speaking in a pretty loud voice and in high pitch.

"Please listen to me and listen carefully, I am the culprit, because of whom the pious *Parubhumi*, our Motherland, is now under menace and people of *Parubhumi* too are facing death threat" Kala continued.

Parjanya and Kadrula were looking at Kala astounded, they just couldn't make out what was happening but the bearded man was listening and looking at Kala as if he knew what Kala is going to confess.

Yes, it's me who followed the *Walahas* that night when they had left for their annual journey. I had committed that sin. I, myself. Please forgive me, if you can", Kalawas full of tears. But he continued with sheer determination,

"Now listen to me in the name of Holy *Parubhumi*, and in the name of the Holy Fire, you all would just do what I say and would do it at once" Kala's voice was touching the sky then. And before anyone could understand anything, in a blink Kala shouted..

"R... U... N... O... V... E... R... M... E..."
Screaming this, Kala right away jumped and threw himself into the witch grass, with his full body stretched and spread himself over the witch grass.

The witch grass promptly got into action with its infamous loud screams tchi tchi tchi.
And so was the old bearded man! Without wasting a single moment, the bearded man ran over Kala and crossed the small witch grass patch and got on the other side, the witch grass had started engulfing Kala quickly.

Very next moment Kadrula got back to senses and he hastily pushed Parjanya who still was not in his senses and was standing like a rock with his eyes wide open.

Kadrula pulled Parjanya and ran after the bearded man, calling for Parjanya.

"Run... Parjanya... Run..."

And in spur of a moment, he came into his sense, Parjanya too ran after Kadrula.

Kala was toiling hard to keep his head high; keeping his both hands and legs high as much as possible to provide the runners the valuable surface and ground clearance. It was the bravest ending act from a son of *Parubhumi*.

All the three men successfully crossed that patch in quick succession and reached on the other side. All that had happened in few seconds only.

But upon reaching there, they saw and realised the value of bravery and sacrifice of Kala.
Each strand of the witch grass was crushing and engulfing Kala and Kala still was trying to make dying efforts to keep his arms and head high. Kala didn't actually know that his sacrifice had done it. But finally the witch grass completely engulfed Kala with its discordant sound Tchi.... Tchi... Tchi....

CHAPTER TWENTY-TWO

Tchi... Tchi.... Tchi... This was the loudest ever sound the witch grass would ever have made.

Kadrula and Parjanya were standing still watching Kala, their eyes were flowing with tears. It was all so much sudden that they couldn't take it. The bearded man came to him and put his each hand on the shoulders of both Kadrula and Parjanya one by one and said "Let's make Kala's sacrifice work now". Both Kadrula and Parjanya turned back towards the village.

It was pretty clear to Kadrula and Parjanya that the current Tchi.. Tchi... Tchi... sound wasn't at all of threatening, as both of them had heard that threatening sound for days and knew that this was a commotion sound of grass due to deadly fear only. And the reason was the Holy Fire that had entered *Parubhumi* again.

Three of them started moving towards the village quickly. It was evening now. The witch grass had almost engulfed half of the village from all the directions but still the centre of the village was untouched.

Kadrula and Parjanya's hearts were cut into pieces viewing all this. They both, when left, the scenario was different and now they were seeing quite disastrous scenario there. Number of houses, trees and vegetations were no more now. While walking quickly, Kadrula, for a moment, looked at one structure similar to a house. It was his home which was now completely engulfed and covered entirely with the witch grass. Parjanya looked at Kadrula with some sympathy, but Kadrula, as if nothing had happened, smiled and crossed it.

And there it was! All the living objects, humans and animals of *Parubhumi* were clubbed together in a considerably smaller and confined area. They all were crammed in.

Everyone was either asleep or fainted; due to the darkness, it was difficult to identify who was who.

All the livestock cow, sheep, goats, buffaloes etc were lifeless but yet looking at the Trio.

They were in a better condition than the humans apparently.

Kadrula noticed some movement to his left and he immediately ran there. Parjanya also followed him. It was Viraj.

"Virajla.. Virajla.. I am Kadrula, this is Parjanya, we are back, we are back with the Holy Fire" Kadrula told to Virajla with much much agony.

Virajla tried to look up but was unable to keep his eyes open. He tried to speak but he couldn't either.

Kadrula and Parjanya got on the job immediately. They started examining people one by one and they found that all were alive but it was due to the ill effects of the witch grass that they were almost lifeless.

And there it was!

The very famous and pious smell of *Siruha*!

The bearded man was holding it burning and he had burnt it in great volume.

Now Kadrula and Parjanya understood what the bearded man was carrying in his arm bag all through the journey. They both were looking to the bearded man with high amount of gratefulness.

The shoulder bag the bearded man was carrying was full of *Siruha.* Even Kadrula, in his entire life, had not seen this much *Siruha* at one place.

The bearded man handed it over to Parjanya to spread the Holy smoke all around.
In a while, Virajla came there fully in his senses as Parjanya had gone to him very first and fast.

Virajla bowed at the feet of the bearded man and he looked at the Holy Fire and his eyes immediately got filled with tears.

"The Last strand of *Siruha* got depleted yesterday morning only, hence we all were helpless and so surrendered to the witch grass evil effect as it had grown stronger and stronger with its intrusion" Virajla told to Kadrula.

"No one of us has had water for the last three days. We just have survived with help of the plants and medicinal fruits brought by you all, Kadrula" there were acute emotions of gratitude in Virajla's voice. "I have seen all our people as well as animals surrendering the witch grass effect one by one and it was so much painful to witness that. I would never forget that till life" he further said.

"Not to worry now, the Holy Fire is here now" the bearded man said as if was keen to punish the witch grass then.

And then, Virajla immediately joined Parjanya, in spreading the pious *Siruha* smoke and smell all around.

And after sometime, among the first who got their sense back and came there were, Neharla and Jhanula. They both bowed at the feet of the bearded man. Life was being spread quite quickly all around and one by one people were coming back to their senses. They were coming to the light of the Holy Fire held by the bearded man.

Everyone who came into senses would come there, bow to the bearded man and to the Holy Fire and would stand aside quietly.

Vasudha was putting in so much effort to hold herself back and not running and hugging Parjanya after she saw her man back victorious. Parjanya just looked at her once and smiled and that one sight and smile confirmed Vasudha with everything she was looking for.

The bearded man then started walking towards the Holy Stones field. He was walking as if he was very much familiar with every inch of that land.

He went up there to one of the very ordinary stones and after walking circularly around, stood there for a while.

Then he closed his eyes and started chanting the holy hymns.

And only then, there was commotion and agitation in the witch grass all around unlike ever before. Tchi.. Tchi..Tchi.. noise was at its highest peak and panic ever.

The bearded man then moved that stone and put the Holy Fire as if re-establishing it there. He then sat in front of it and closed his eyes again and continued chanting the Holy chants.

For quite long time the bearded man remained so.

Finally he opened his eyes, took up the Holy Fire in both of his hands and started walking towards the witch grass.

There was now the commotion of deadly feeling in the witch grass then.

Tchi.. Tchi.. Tchi.. was all around as if touching the sky now.

The witch grass of two men's height, started leaning backwards to stay away from the Holy fire.

The bearded man stopped for a while, and then, while chanting the holy chants he touched the flame of Holy Fire to the witch grass.

And, at once, the Holy fire as if engulfing, started burning out the witch grass rapidly.

Tchi...Tchi...Tchi... was now apparently the painful sound, it was fainting every moment as well.

The Holy Fire spread all around in an eye blink time, they all were in the middle of *Parubhumi*, in the centre, and the fire was all around them.

And within few moments, there was a silence! A complete silence, the silence that the people of *Parubhumi* didn't have for last so many days.

The bearded man walked back to the Holy Stones field.

There was a happiness and human voices expressing joy all around now.

Even the Animals had started making sound of happiness and life.

"It is over now. One of your own people broke the rule of *Parubhumi* and so this had happened. He had sacrificed himself for his Motherland however. But now you all should learn from this. Respect the rules of *Parubhumi*, and law of Nature and you will be flourishing for generations" the bearded man briefly addressed the people of *Parubhumi*.

And all the people of *Parubhumi* at once bowed to him.

"And now it is time for me to leave as well" said the bearded man.

"But this is your land, you can't go" Neharla came forward, bowed to the bearded man, and said.

"Yes that is true but I have to go and that is also as per the rule" the bearded man said smilingly and started walking.

And suddenly someone came there and collapsed at the feet of the bearded man.
Everyone was surprised. The bearded man too stopped walking and looked down at the person at his feet.

That was Shivala! Shivala joined both his hands to the bearded man and was trying to say something but was unable to, as always.

"Oh Shiva... Shivala... yes, I forgive you" said the bearded man promptly.

And he kept looking at Shivala. Shivala still was trying hard to say something but couldn't. Then after few moments of the silence, the bearded man again said "Okay, as you please, I free you from the curse as well" saying this, the bearded man touched the head of Shivala with his one hand and started walking again.

And at the very next moment, Shivalal laid down on the ground!

Everyone was astonished. Two Great men had left the *Parubhumi* in that eternal moment...